THE PAY-OFF

FINALLY I said okay, I'd do what she asked, and she said, "I'll get Number One to see you" . . . and I said, "Are you one of his real close friends?" and she said, "Why? *Jealous?*" and I said why the hell should I be jealous, and she said, "Maybe because you go for me," and I said I'd be a damn liar if I said I didn't—and the next time what was more I was going all the way. . . .

The Hot Shot

Fletcher Flora

PROLOGUE BOOKS

F + W Media, Inc.

Published in electronic format by
PROLOGUE BOOKS
an imprint of F+W Media, Inc.
10151 Carver Road
Blue Ash, Ohio 45242
www.prologuebooks.com

eISBN 10: 1-4405-3905-7
eISBN 13: 978-1-4405-3905-3
POD ISBN 10: 1-4405-5621-0
POD ISBN 13: 978-1-4405-5621-0

This is a work of fiction. Names, characters, corporations, institutions,
organizations, events, or locales in this novel are either the product of the author's
imagination or, if real, used fictitiously. The resemblance of any character to actual
persons (living or dead) is entirely coincidental.

This work has been previously published in print format by:
Avon Publications, Inc., New York, NY.

Part I: *DEAR OLD HIGH*

MY OLD MAN was a bum, and my old lady was a slob, and chances are I'd be a slob and a bum both if it wasn't for this God-damn crazy game.

Funny thing is, I didn't intend to play it. The way I got started was just one of those things. I was walking down the hall of the high school past the gym, and to tell the truth, I was thinking about going down to Beegie's pool room to pick up a few nickels playing rotation, but the door to the gym was open, and I just happened to look in while I was passing, and there was this guy I knew, name of Bugs, running around with all these other guys throwing a ball at a hoop. I gave old Bugs a hoot and a holler, and thumbed my nose at him, and he thumbed back and yelled for me to come on in, so I did, and I don't know why.

You weren't supposed to walk on the gym floor in your street shoes, so I went along the edge back to where Bugs was standing, and I asked him what the hell he was doing playing around with sissy stuff like that, and he said it wasn't so God-damn sissy when you got into it, and he'd bet two-bits I couldn't throw the ball through the hoop two times out of ten if I'd stand back where he told me to stand. It didn't seem to me to make a hell of a lot of difference whether I could throw the ball through the hoop two times out of ten or ten times out of ten, but old Bugs was so snotty about it, putting up his lousy two-bits that way, that I decided I'd take the bet, and besides, it was faster than five games of rotation. I saw how the other guys were sort of pushing the ball up toward the hoop with one hand, sometimes jumping up in the air a little when they did it, so Bugs got a ball and tossed it to me and told me where to stand, and I pushed it up the way I saw the others doing it, and damned if it didn't go through. Bugs just hooted and said it was plain pig luck and I couldn't do it again if I tried all day, so I pushed the ball up nine more times, and as a matter

5

of fact, it went through the hoop seven times altogether. All the other guys were standing around watching me by that time, and they razzed Bugs pretty good, and Bugs said he'd pay off the next time he saw me at Beegie's, and I said the hell he would, he'd pay off right now.

It was just about then that someone said, "Skimmer! Skimmer Scaggs!" and the truth is, he said it so sudden and so close to my shoulder that it scared the hell out of me. I turned around to see who it was, and it was this spook Mulloy, coach of the team, and he'd sneaked up behind me on his Goddamn rubber-soled shoes. He was a big guy going kind of bald and with a lot of flab around the belly, even if he was athletic as hell and all that, and he was one of these man-to-man scoutmaster kind of bastards. I thought at first he was going to tell me to get the hell off the floor with my street shoes on, but it turned out he'd been watching me from the beginning and had something else on his mind. He started out telling me I ought to be ashamed of myself, and then he switched off on a sermon about how everyone owed something to the dear old school, and the more you had to offer, the more you owed, because it was the duty of the gifted to give a full measure of their gifts, and to make it short, I finally began to get the idea that I was gifted at throwing a ball through a hoop and was some kind of dirty son of a bitch because I hadn't been out there in the gym doing it a long time ago instead of hanging around Beegie's all the time, and altogether it was the kind of crap to make you puke. I was on the verge of telling old Mulloy to blow it, but then I happened to look around and see the faces of the other guys, and I didn't say it.

I might as well tell the truth about it. The truth is, I wasn't very popular around school, and I'd been thinking pretty hard about putting the place down for good and all, but now I saw these guys standing there with their teeth hanging out and a kind of old buddy-buddy look in their eyes, and I began to get the drift that I'd made a lot of points just by throwing that damn ball through the hoop seven times out of ten with no practice, and I began to think, What the hell, why not, a guy never knows when he can use a few suckers on his side. It was pretty plain these guys really swallowed the bull old Mul-

6

loy put out, and one of them, a tall skinny creep who wore contact lenses plastered on his eyeballs, spoke up and said that the team sure could use a sharpshooter like me, and everyone hoped I'd play, and as a matter of fact, this creep was Tizzy Davis, whose old man was president of the Farmers and Merchants Bank, and the whole family was snotty as the window in a nursery. Well, in the end I told a lot of God-damn lies about how I'd always wanted to play and had started to try out for the team two or three times but never had because I figured I wouldn't be any good at it, and old buller Mulloy put an arm around my shoulders so I got a good whiff of his lousy stinking sweat shirt that smelled like my old man's underwear, and he said in one of these loud jovial voices, "Skimmer, you get in that locker room and get a suit and a pair of shoes and get back out here for practice. Fellows, I got an idea Skimmer's just the fellow we've been looking for."

I went in the locker room and put on a suit and a pair of basketball shoes, and I felt pretty naked because I didn't have a jock strap. I was supposed to have one for gym class, but I didn't have it because I never went to the damn class, in spite of their threatening to throw me out of school for not going, and that was because all they ever did in gym class was a lot of corny squats and push-ups and stuff that didn't amount to anything but plain hard work, and I couldn't see any percentage in it. Anyhow, I decided I'd have to have a jock strap if I was going to play basketball in public, and I went back out and we played some, and I guess I just had the knack for it, because it turned out that I was pretty damn good. Every once in a while old Mulloy would stop us and show me how to catch the ball and pass it and a lot of stuff about pivoting and dribbling and things like that, and at first I just wished he'd let me the hell alone so I could throw the ball through the hoop, but after a while I was damn glad to have him stop us any time he wanted to, because the truth is, it pooped me out running up and down the damn court. He had us play what he called a firehorse game, and I learned later this was just the opposite of what was called a control game, which meant the teams that played a control game sort of took their time when they had the ball and tried to set up plays for good shots and all, while we just grabbed the ball and raced like hell for the

7

basket that was ours and slammed away at it with the idea that the ball was bound to go through enough times to win the game if you tried often enough. As a matter of fact, it hadn't been going through so often, though, and that's why they wanted a sharpshooter like me, but to tell the truth, in the beginning I wished to hell we played a control game ourselves.

We kept at it so God-damn long I began to think, To hell with it, I wish I'd gone on down to Beegie's and played rotation, and before we were through I began to get sick in the belly, and I thought I was going to puke right there on the lousy floor, but then we quit and went in the locker room and had showers, and old Mulloy came out of his little cubbyhole of an office and had a shower too, and stood around all manly and naked and calling everyone fellow until you wanted to poke him right in his fat mouth, and he wound up saying, "Skimmer, old man, we're going to make the best dog-gone forward in the state out of you, and I'm predicting right now that this little old team is going to win the league championship and then go right on to take the state tournament. How about it, fellows?"

They all laughed and yelled like a bunch of boobs and said sure, that was right, and slapped each other on the bare butt, and no one but Tizzy Davis himself came over and sat down on the bench beside me and said, "Sure glad you've joined us, Scaggs. You're a natural." Then he gave me one of these damn virile slaps on the bare shoulders, and it stung like hell, the skinny fruit, and if it'd been anyone else I'd have knocked him on his ass, but as it was I let it go, and he stood up and said, "By the way, Scaggs, you ought to get together with some of us fellows some evening. We have some damn good times."

He said damn like it was something he just threw in to show what a hell of a guy he was underneath and I almost spit in his eyes, it was so damn funny, but it didn't turn out to be so funny after all, and a lot of those so-called nice guys really *were* a lot different underneath than you'd think to watch the prissy way they talked and carried on. That went for Tizzy Davis in spades, and I'm ashamed to say that right while I was talking to him that first time there in the locker room, I was a stinking virgin and he wasn't.

8

After I was dressed, I went out with Bugs, and old Mulloy yelled after me that practice was at three o'clock sharp tomorrow afternoon, and I said sure, I'd be there, and Bugs said, "Boy, you're solid. This game is the nuts."

"Nuts is right," I said, and he said, "No bull, Skimmer, this God-damn game's a racket. You don't have to study a damn bit, and you still pass all your subjects, because the coach runs down to the principal and raises blue hell if any of the team flunks, and the principal goes and raises hell with the teacher that flunked you, because the principal thinks the team is great stuff for school spirit and all that crap, and he won't stand for any of the guys being flunked."

I said I didn't study, anyhow, and didn't need any crummy excuse like playing a crummy game to keep me from doing it, and he said sure, that was right, but as it was I flunked half my subjects at least and this way I wouldn't flunk any at all, because anyone that flunked couldn't play on the team. "Besides," he said, "that's not all of it," and I said, "What's the rest of it?" and he said, "Well, the dolls, for one thing," and I said, "What the hell about the dolls?" and he said, "Jesus, Skimmer, the dolls really go for the guys that play this game. No bull, you're a hotshot if you're on the team. You'd think throwing that ball around made you some kind of lousy hero or something. You got to be on some kind of team to get the real classy dolls."

"I haven't seen you with any real classy dolls lately," I said, and he said, "Never mind. I got a couple sniffing at me. You just wait and see. You won't have to fool around any more with old Mopsy Beacon once the classy dolls get an eyeful of you giving your all for the dear old school," and I said, "Jesus Christ, you sound just like that God-damn Mulloy. Besides, what's the matter with Mopsy Beacon? Ever since Mopsy told her old man you tried to sneak a feel, and he told your old man and got the hell beat out of you, you've had a hard on for her. You start riding Mopsy again, I'm liable to give you a fat lip."

"You and who else?" he said, and I stopped and said, "You like to find out?" and he gave this sickly laugh and said, "Oh, to hell with Mopsy. She's just a ring-tailed wonder. Ava Gardner's just a hag compared to Mopsy."

9

I let it drop then, because I really didn't want to slap old Bugs around any, him being a pretty good guy for a God-damn moron, and besides, to tell the truth, Mopsy wasn't worth it. She wasn't a bad looking doll when she took her crummy goggles off, and if I'd wanted to I could've told Bugs that she might have squealed on him for sneaking a feel, but she didn't squeal on me, and I'd done it lots of times, but the hell of it was, she wouldn't let me go any farther. You tried to get down to business, she started telling you all this bull about how that was something holy and precious that ought to be saved till after a guy and a girl were married, and I got sore once and told her that if she was planning to save it that long for me, she'd be saving it forever.

Bugs and I had to go through town to get over on the side where we lived, which was the crummy side, naturally, and on the way we passed Dummke's Cigar Store. When we got in front of it, I told Bugs to give me the lousy two-bits he owed me because I was all out of cigarettes and wanted to get some. He started in telling me how I couldn't smoke any more, now that I was on the team, because cigarettes took your wind, and wind was one of the most important things when it came to playing basketball, and I said he was just trying to get out of paying off the two-bits, and I didn't intend to give up gaspers for any lousy game, and pretty soon he dug down in his stinking pocket and paid off, only twenty-three cents, though, three nickels and eight God-damn pennies. If there's anything I hate, it's pennies, because you always feel like a damn fool counting them out, and whoever's selling you whatever you're buying keeps looking at you like you were a crummy cheap-skate who'd robbed the baby's piggy bank or something, and besides, someone's always saying, "You got a penny for tax?" and if you don't have it, they say, "Oh, that's all right, I'll get it next time," but if you do have it, you got to fork the damn thing over, and you always feel like a sucker for having it.

Twenty-three cents was just exactly enough for the cig-arettes, so I went in to get them, and old Gravy Dummke him-self came up behind the counter to wait on me. Everyone called him Gravy because he got a cut from so God-damn many crooked things around town, and it was a crying wonder how he did it, because you wouldn't have thought to look at him

10

that anyone would have bothered to spit on him. He was fat and greasy with a headful of dirty black curls all slopped up with some kind of stinking oil, and when he smiled at you it looked like his whole damn face fell apart and left you standing there looking at about a square mile of ivory. The smile didn't mean a damn thing, though, and he was a nasty bastard, always throwing something into you and breaking it off, and today he said, "Hello, kid. You still out of jail?"

"You're a hell of a one to be yakking about jail," I said. "The cop'll jump that game in your back room someday, and you'll damn well think jail."

His fat, greasy face smoothed out like a billiard ball, and his little eyes got kind of sleepy and mean, and he said, "You got a big mouth, kid. You're bound to get in big trouble someday, you got such a big mouth."

I said, "All I want is a God-damn pack of cigarettes. You want to sell me a pack of cigarettes or not?" and he said, "Why the hell should I particularly want to sell you a lousy pack of cigarettes?" but he slapped a pack on the counter, anyhow, the brand I smoked, and I slapped all those stinking pennies on the glass counter and spread them around and left. You ever tried to pick up a lot of coins off a glass counter? It's a hell of a job.

Outside, Bugs said, "You oughtn't to needle Gravy that way. Gravy's a pretty damn big shot, if you want to know it. Jackie Bramble's big brother works for Gravy, dealing and taking bets and things like that, and he says Gravy's got connections in the city with all the big gamblers and everyone," and I said, "He's just a lousy small-town punk, and if he had so much on the ball he'd be a big shot gambler up in the city himself instead of being down here in this jerk town running a crummy game in the back of a cigar store. Besides, it wouldn't make any difference if he had connections with Frank Costello himself, I don't take any lip from any lousy greaseball."

We went on through town, and the lights were on because it was getting late and it got dark pretty early that time of year, and I thought about hanging around for a while before I went home, but I didn't do it because all the damn running up and down had made me hungry as hell, and I didn't

11

have any money to buy a hamburger or anything with. The farther we walked, the crummier it got, and when it got just about as crummy as it was going to get, that's where I lived. Bugs turned off to cross over a few blocks to the street he lived on, and he said he'd see me tomorrow at school, and I said sure, I'd see him around, and I kept on going down the street I was on to the house I lived in, and it was dark as hell down there and pretty cold.

I went up across the porch and back through the house to the kitchen, and the old man and the old lady were still bellied up to the table, and the old man said, "Where the hell you been?"

I said, "I been playing basketball, if you want to know, that's where I've been," and he said, "Basketball? What the hell you mean, basketball?" and I said, "I mean basketball, that's what I mean. Didn't you ever hear of basketball?"

He laid his knife down on the table and wiped his mouth with the back of his hand and looked at me like he was stupid, which he was. "By God, I can't believe I heard right," he said, and I said, "You dig the muck out of your ears, maybe you could hear better."

He glared at me across the table and said, "Don't mouth off at me, you smart little bastard, and I'll tell you something else too. No kid of mine is going to play any God-damn silly games, and you get home for your supper on time after this or I'll damn well go up the side of your head."

"I'll play any games I like, and I won't ask you a damn thing about it before I do," I said, but I said it too close, and the old man jumped up and clobbered me on the side of the head before I could duck. He was pretty strong in spite of being a beer-soaked slob, and he slammed me up against the wall and damn near knocked my brains out. That set the old lady to bawling, and she went into the old routine about how I was a bad boy, and it was all because I'd lost the big brother I needed to look after me and teach me what I needed to know, but that was a lot of bull because my big brother, whose name was Eddie, hadn't ever loked after me any at all, and the only things he ever taught me were some dirty stories and limericks and how to shoot pool. He'd been in the war and off in some

12

stinking place like New Guinea or somewhere, and he'd written me this letter once that said pretty plain between the lines that he was damn sick of it and was going to pull out and desert the first chance he got, but damned if he didn't get killed before he could go. That made the old lady a gold star war mother or something corny like that, and she sure as hell got her kicks out of it, especially when she was drunk.

After my head quit ringing, I eased into my chair at the table and began to eat, and the chow was pretty damn lousy, besides being cold, and the only reason I bothered to eat at all was because I'd worked up this big appetite. Pretty soon the old man got up and said he was going up the street to the tavern to watch the fights, and I said if he'd quit blowing all his money for beer in the lousy tavern he'd have enough to buy a television set, and we could all watch the God-damn fights. He looked like he was figuring to clobber me again, but he hardly ever bothered to clobber me more than once a day, and so he just belched and rubbed his fat gut and went on out. I finished eating and went in the living room and sat down and tried to think of something to do with the damn night. There wasn't any use going back uptown, because I didn't have any money, and I'd had plenty of Bugs for one day, a little of Bugs going a hell of a long way, and finally I decided I might as well go over and see if I could stir up something with Mopsy, so I went.

The whole damn sky was lousy with stars, and the moon was floating around big and yellow up there among them, and when you walked under a tree and looked up you could see the moon and a big mess of the stars through the bare branches of the tree, and it was like seeing it all through a God-damn black filigree or something, and it was a pretty good eyeful if you cared for that kind of crap. The wind was blowing pretty strong in the street, stirring up the dead leaves in the yards and along the gutter, and it was damn cold, and I got to thinking that it was too cold to sit outside with Mopsy, and what the hell could you do with Mopsy inside with her old man and her old lady hanging around, and I was about to turn around and go home and to hell with it when it occurred to me that there was an outside chance that the old man and the old

13

lady had gone out to a movie or somewhere, and so I took the chance and went on, and that's just the way it turned out, as luck would have it.

Mopsy opened the door when I knocked, and I said, "Hi, Mopsy," and I could tell by the way she looked half glad and half scared, like she knew damn well she was going to do something she wasn't supposed to do, that no one was home but her.

"Hi, Skimmer," she said. "What are you doing here?"

I said, "I just came over to do a little diddling," and she said, "Don't you talk like that, Skimmer. Besides, you can't come in. Mom and Pop are gone to the movies, and I can't have boys in the house when they're gone."

"Nuts," I said. "Who's going to know besides us? I'll get the hell out before they come back."

"Well," she said, "they'll be back around nine, so you'll have to leave by eight-thirty."

"Sure," I said. "I'll be gone like Callahan," and I went in.

She had her goggles off and her hair pushed up on top of her head and pinned there, and the fact was, she looked pretty good, sort of sophisticated, if you know what I mean, except she was too heavy, not really fat but damn plump, and she was wearing these crummy saddleshoes and white sox instead of high heels and nylons like any smart doll wears when she wants to send a guy. She was stacked up good, though, even if she did pack a little too much altogether, and her tail had a nice little wobble to it when she walked. I sat down on the sofa and watched her wobble it over to the radio-phonograph, and she said, "You want to hear some music?" and I said, "Sure. Put on a stack."

She started the first platter spinning and came back and sat down beside me on the sofa, and I began to think that she was just the soft-headed kind that would be impressed all to hell by something like a guy playing on the school basketball team, so I said, "I'll bet you can't guess what I've been doing," and she said, "No, what?"

"Playing basketball," I said.

"Basketball?" she said.

"Hell, yes, basketball," I said. "Can't you understand anything?"

"Where you been playing basketball?" she said, and I said,

14

"I been playing at school. Where the hell else is there to play basketball?"

"On the team?" she said.

"God Almighty, yes, on the team," I said. "You think you play basketball all by yourself or something?"

By that time her eyes were sort of shining, and her mouth was hanging open a little like she was in heat, and she said, "Oh, Skimmer, that's wonderful," and I could see that she was already thinking about me being a school big shot, maybe, and dragging her around to dances and places with me, and I thought, Fat chance, sister, if everything old Bugs said about the classy dolls turns out to be true. Meantime, though, I was making a hell of a lot of points, and old Mopsy wasn't too damn bad while I was waiting for something better, and as a matter of fact, we wound up doing a lot of kissing and having a pretty hot tussle there on the sofa, and if I hadn't had to clear out at eight-thirty—except it was almost nine before I left— I got an idea I might even have got past that holy and precious stuff she always came up with at the last minute. Anyhow, on the way home I decided that if it worked like that on Mopsy there wasn't any reason why it shouldn't work on a lot of others, and I made up my mind right then and there to give this basketball crap the big try, and I didn't worry any about the old man's guff about no kid of his playing, either, because he didn't really give a damn what the hell I did, or if I ever came home for supper on time or any other time, and he'd only stirred up a brawl over it tonight because he was handy and felt like raising hell.

I did it too. I went for it whole hog. I got me a jock strap and went out for practice every God-damn afternoon after school and sometimes on Saturday, and I guess I ran up and down that court damn near a million miles, and as a matter of fact, old Bugs was right, and I had to ease up on the gaspers some, but I didn't quit entirely as a matter of principle. Old Mulloy would make me stand back on the outside of the keyhole, which means the black lines painted on the floor in front of the basket that look like a big keyhole, and he'd stand in the keyhole under the basket and fire the God-damn ball out to me and yell, "Jump and push," and I'd jump and push the ball at the basket, and he'd grab it and fire it back like the son

15

of a bitch was hot and yell, "Jump and push," and I'd jump
and push again, and after a while he'd have old Tizzy Davis
stand in there under the basket and fire the ball out, because
Tizzy was center, and it was really his job, and before long I got
free and fancy and loose as ashes and could flip the ball
through the net almost every time with a little swish, and it was
just like shooting a lot of God-damn fish in a rain barrel.

Like I said, old Tizzy played center, being so tall and skinny
and sort of limber, and the idea was to slam the ball to him
under the basket, and if he had a chance he was supposed to
jump up and away from whoever was guarding him and hook
the ball over into the basket—only the other guys called it a
bucket instead of a basket, and I got to calling it that too—
and if he didn't have the chance to hook the ball in, he was
supposed to fire it back to me outside the keyhole, and I was
supposed to throw it through from there, and I don't mind
saying it worked damned good. As a matter of fact, you've
got to give the devil his due, and there weren't any flies on old
Tizzy when it came to playing that pivot position, which is
what we called it, and the only thing wrong with him was
that every once in a while he'd lose one of those God-damn
contact lenses off his eyeball, and then we'd all have to stop
and go crawling all over the lousy floor until someone found it.

We always wound up every practice with the first team playing the second team, and I was on the first team right off,
and old Bugs was on the second team. As a matter of fact, he
played guard and was supposed to keep me from making any
points, and I really gave the poor bastard a hard time, and before we finished playing his tail was always rubbing out his
tracks. Old Mulloy would stand along the side, sometimes running up and down a little, and he'd keep yelling, "Run, run,
run! Move, move move! Pass that ball, pass that ball!" Once
in a while he'd run out on the court waving his arms around
to stop the action and chew somebody out for not doing something the way he should've done it, but he never called it
chewing out because he didn't go for cussing, and once when
I did a little in a natural sort of way, damned if he didn't give
me a five-minute lecture on sportsmanship and clean speech,
the son of a bitch, when all the time he wasn't interested in
anything, really, but running the hell out of you, and he didn't

16

give a damn if you dropped dead just as long as he won his God-damn games.

We came up pretty close to the time for our first game, and along about then I had some trouble with a God-damn old grandma named Cupper. He taught geometry in the school, and if you've ever tried the stuff you'll understand what God-awful tripe it is, and I'd taken it once before and hadn't done any good with it, and now I was taking it again, because I had to, and I wasn't doing any better this time, and as a matter of fact, I wasn't doing a damn thing. Anyhow, old Cupper got wind of my playing basketball, and he served notice on the coach that there wasn't any way on God's earth I could make a passing mark in geometry, and that I couldn't play, and old Mulloy just hit the God-damn ceiling and went screaming down to the principal. I got called down to the office later, and the principal and the coach and old Cupper were all there, and you could tell they'd been raising hell because the principal was red in the face, and he kept taking off and putting on these fancy goggles with a black ribbon on them, and the coach was red in the face too, but old Cupper was white as a sheet, so I figured the principal and the coach had been dishing it out, and old Cupper had been taking it. He looked like he was about a hundred years old, and he had a little gray curl that hung down over his forehead, and these God-damn plates kept clacking around in his mouth. Take it from me, he was so damn dry it made you thirsty to look at him, but maybe it was what you'd expect in a guy who'd spent most of his lousy life teaching something as dry as geometry.

Well, the principal had me sit in a chair just like the rest of them, which surprised the hell out of me, and he started in telling me what great things he'd heard about me from old Mulloy, and what a fine thing he thought it was for a young man to serve his school so well, and I knew he was just breaking it off in old Cupper, but he lost control of himself and overdid it, and I kept remembering some of the other things he'd told me at different times, and it was confusing as hell, and I had a feeling generally that he was talking about someone else. He wound up saying there had been a little misunderstanding, but he was sure everything could be worked out all right and that Mr. Cupper wouldn't want to do anything to hurt the

17

team, and old Cupper broke in with his voice trembling and said that nothing could ever be worked out unless Scaggs, meaning me, did a little work himself, and then the principal got mean as hell and said right out that Scaggs, meaning me again, would receive a passing mark in geometry or else someone, meaning old Cupper, would suffer the God-damn consequences, only he didn't say God-damn. Old Cupper got so excited that his teeth began to rattle like a hot crap game. The truth is, I felt kind of sorry for the damn old fool, but I wasn't going to louse anything up by saying so. What's more, I had a sneaky feeling he was right, and if I'd been him and he'd been me, I wouldn't have given him nothing, but nothing. Not that God-damn Mulloy, though. That righteous bastard didn't feel sorry for anyone ever, and all the way back to the locker room he kept crowing like a banty rooster about how it was time certain people were learning that there was more went into the making of a man than what came out of a crummy book.

The night of the first game finally came around, and I might as well come right out and admit it, I was as nervous as a whore in church. It was a home game, and I'd never been to see a damn game before, even though I was a senior and was there my fourth year, and to tell the truth, I was surprised at the big fuss they made over it. Man, the God-damn place was jumping. All the seats were full up in the sections where people were supposed to sit, and they brought in a lot of folding chairs and set them up around the sides of the court, except where the benches for the teams were, and the school band sat down at one end of the gym just off the court and played all these snappy marches that are enough to make you get your rocks off, and all the time these crazy guys in white pants and dolls in little white pleated skirts ran up and down on the court and jumped in the air and waved their arms and yelled, "Fifteen for the team, fifteen for the team," and everyone, even the ones old enough to know better, jumped up and yelled fifteen rahs in batches of twos and threes with three big teams after them, and in my opinion they all acted like God-damn maniacs.

The game finally got started, and I guess all the rest of the team were as nervous as I was, because every time we got hold of the ball we threw the damn thing away, and the only good thing was that the other team was even worse than we were. After a while, though, someone managed to get the ball in to old Tizzy, and Tizzy banged it out to me, and I banged it through, and you'd have thought from the racket that went up that I'd won a war all by myself or something. After that, we settled down, and I could hear old Mulloy yelling, "Run, run, run!" and we ran like hell, and I'm telling you straight that the other team didn't have a sucker's chance from then on. We really ran the pants off the poor bastards. They must not have been so hot, anyhow, to tell the truth, because they finally wound up in the cellar at the end of the season, but it was a damn good game to get us started off on top, especially me, because I got hotter than a bitch in August and scored thirty points altogether. To tell the honest truth, it would have been better sometimes if I'd passed back in to Tizzy under the basket, because he'd broken free of his guard and could have laid it in like nothing, but you don't make points for number one that way, and besides, I was hitting the bucket myself, so what the hell. The God-damn goofy creeps up in the seats and all around the floor in the folding chairs kept yelling, "Scaggs, Scaggs, Scaggs!" and once, during a time out that the other team took to suck their guts in, the guys and dolls in white pants and white shirts got out on the floor and got everyone to yell fifteen rahs with three Scaggses after them, and I'm bound to say it gave me a funny feeling in spite of myself to hear my name yelled out like that. Nothing like that had ever happened to me before, or any other Scaggs, either, for that matter, except in a kind of way to Eddie when the paper printed his name as a war hero, but he was dead then and couldn't appreciate it. And incidentally, the guys who led the yells weren't the only ones who wore white pants. The girls did too, and you could see them when they jumped up in the air and made their skirts fly up, and I thought myself that it was a better show than the God-damn game.

In the locker room after it was all over, everyone was yelling and horse-playing and acting as wild as a pregnant fox in a forest fire, and no one but the principal himself came in and shook my hand and said, "Congratulations on a great game, Scaggs," and I was naked at the time and felt silly as hell. Old Mulloy kept prancing up and down the room in the steam and

19

stink, taking big breaths of the air like it was blowing over roses and sticking his God-damn chest out like Tarzan, and he kept saying, "Great game, fellows, great game," but then he'd stop and say, "Don't let it go to your heads, though. There's a lot of kinks in this team, a lot of kinks, and it's going to take a lot of work to get them out," and it was pretty plain that he was trying to give the impression that he was about the only God-damn coach on earth who could do it. It all got pretty pukey, to tell the truth, especially the horseplay, and while I was in the shower old Tizzy Davis reached around inside with one of those skinny arms of his that were about as long as an ape's and turned the hot water off and damn near froze my tail. I never did go for that kind of stuff much, and I was about to go out and slap his stinking chops for him, but then I decided if I was going to mess around with this bunch of goof-balls I'd have to learn to take that kind of kid stuff, and I might as well start now, so I didn't do it.

It was a good thing I didn't, and I'll tell you why. When I finally went out of the locker room into the hall, there was old Tizzy talking to a couple of dolls, and he said, "Come on over here, Scaggs. I want you to meet my sister." Well, you could have knocked me over with a feather when I heard him say that, because I was already beginning to get the idea that Bugs had been right about the classy dolls, and some of them were already beginning to look at me that hadn't ever looked at me before, but I'd never expected anything like Tizzy Davis's sister, and that's no bull. Anyhow, I went over there, and Tizzy said, "Marsha, this is Skimmer Scaggs, the best damn forward in the state," and Marsha laughed and said, "Well, it isn't exactly true that Tizzy wanted you to meet me. It's more that I wanted to meet you," and I thought, Oh, oh, hold on to your God-damn hats because here we go.

I said I was glad to meet her, and I was, and that's the truth if I ever told it. She was a junior in school, a year younger than Tizzy and me, and she had this very pale blond hair and this willowy kind of body that looked like it could wrap itself around you and tie a half-hitch, and besides, her voice had this kind of little laugh running through it all the time that made you wonder what the hell she was thinking about, and her eyes, which were blue and kind of shining, came up at you

20

through her lashes with a sly sort of look that made you wonder what they did for entertainment over on the side of town where people like the Davises lived. She was a classy doll, all right, doubled in spades, and I don't mind telling you that I met and had a lot of dolls after her, but there never was a damn one of them a damn bit classier, even in college or the city or places like that.

She said, "Do you have anything in particular to do?" and I said I didn't, and she said, "We're going over to Tompkins' for hamburgers and cokes. Would you like to come?"

I said that sounded pretty good to me, and she said, "Oh, that's wonderful. Don't you think that's wonderful, Tizzy?" Tizzy said he did, and I couldn't tell from his voice whether he really meant it or not, and to tell the truth, I didn't give a damn. We all walked over to Tompkins', Marsha and me behind, and she hung onto my arm real tight, sort of running her hand up and down the inside of it every now and then, and all the time she kept telling me what a wonderful game I'd played, and just to think it was the first real game I'd ever played in my life, and she bet someday I'd be one of the best basketball players in the country and make All-American in *Collier's* and *Look* and all the big magazines and newspapers.

Tompkins' was a joint where all the classy dolls and fancy guys from school hung out, and I'd never been in it before, but tonight I walked in like I owned the place, and the way everyone started yelling Good game, Scaggs, great going, Scaggs, thataboy, Scaggs, they must have thought I owned it too. We got a booth in the back, Tizzy and his girl, name of Marion, on one side and Marsha and me on the other, and we ordered hamburgers and cokes, and I'm ready to swear that was the first time I remembered that I didn't have a God-damn red cent in my pocket. It took some of the fun out of it, that's for sure, because I kept wondering if that damn Tizzy would pick up the check, and what the hell I'd do if he didn't.

There was a juke box jumping in a corner, and Tizzy and his girl got out of the booth to dance, and Marsha said, "Aren't you going to ask me to dance?" and I said, "I don't know much about dancing. I guess I just never bothered to learn," and she said, "Oh, it's easy, there's nothing to it, come on." She grabbed my hand and pulled me out of the booth, and there wasn't a

21

hell of a lot to it, at that, and I had a kind of knack for it, just like I had for basketball. As a matter of fact, I found out I had a knack for a hell of a lot of things I'd never thought anything about, and probably I'd never have found out about any of them if it hadn't been for the day old Bugs called me into the gym and bet me two-bits I couldn't throw the ball through the hoop two times out of ten.

Marsha was a real classy dancer and hardly seemed to touch the floor, she was so light on her feet, but she touched plenty in other places, namely all up and down the front of me, and she kept whispering things to me about how marvelous it was I could pick up the steps so quick and how strange it was she had never noticed me around before, and her lips kept brushing the side of my neck, and it may not seem like much to happen, but it was better than a tussle with old Mopsy on her lousy sofa anytime. We kept on dancing for a long time to the nickels other guys fed the juke box, and when we finally got back to the booth, old Tizzy and his girls were standing up ready to go.

"Wait a minute," I said. "I'd better pay the check," but Tizzy said, "Oh, never mind, I've already paid it," and I said, "You didn't have to do that," and he said, "That's all right," and the truth is, I'd seen him pay it, and that's why I'd come back to the booth.

Outside on the street, old Tizzy said, "Sorry I don't have the old man's car tonight, Scaggs, or I'd drive you home."

I said, "Oh, that's all right," and it was too, because to tell the truth, I didn't much want them to see the crummy dump I lived in, and besides, if the old man and the old lady happened to be in one of their brawls, you could hear them all over the God-damn neighborhood, even with all the doors and windows closed. Anyhow, Marsha spoke up and said, "It's a wonderful night for walking. You go on with Marion, Tizzy, and Skimmer will see I get home. You wouldn't object to walking me home, would you, Skimmer?" She said it with this sly look through her lashes and the kind of little laugh in her voice, like she knew God-damn well no guy with all his marbles would object to walking *her* home, and I wondered for a second what she'd say if I said Hell, yes, I'd object to taking her shank's mare clear the hell across the lousy town, but you can bet I didn't say it, but said instead, "It would be my pleasure," which was pretty damn corny, I admit, but true, nevertheless.

Old Tizzy said all right and went off with his girl Marion, who wasn't a bad piece herself, except she had the kind of teeth you could use to eat roasting ears through a picket fence, and I started off with Marsha across town, not east toward the crummy section where I lived, but north toward the section where the people lived who were lousy with dough, and she held onto my arm and kept running her hand up and down the inside of it like she did before on the way to Tompkins'. She said again she simply couldn't understand how she'd missed me so long around school and asked me to tell her all about myself, because she simply had to know every little detail about a guy who was bound to be a big basketball star and famous as all hell, and I thought, Anytime you think I'm going to louse up the works by telling you about my crummy family, baby, you're a hell of a lot crazier than I think you are, so instead I told her a lot of God-damn lies about how my old man was pretty poor, even though he'd once been on the way to becoming a damn millionaire or something, and this was because he had a very bad disease of some kind that he never talked about and the doctors couldn't do anything about, and it was just a damn crying shame all around. I told her, besides, that my older brother had been killed in the war, which was the only true thing I told her, and that my old lady had been heart-broken ever since and just seemed to keep on wasting away over the grief of it, but as a matter of fact, my old lady never felt any grief in her life that she couldn't cure with a few cans of beer. Anyhow, I got warmed up to it pretty well and laid it on pretty thick, and she kept hanging onto my arm tighter and tighter and rubbing harder and harder on the inside, and every once in a while she'd make this little cooing sound that was like a doll makes when she's working up to a tumble, and by the time I'd finished, damned if we hadn't walked all the way across to her neighborhood and down to her house on the very street she lived on.

It was a big God-damn place, built like one of these old colonial mansions you see in pictures about the Civil War and stuff, and it was set back of a big front yard with a lot of trees

23

and bushes growing around and a curved driveway going up one side and around in front of the house. We stopped along the drive under a tree, and she said, "I'm sorry I can't ask you to come in tonight. You understand, don't you?" and I thought, Sure, I understand. I understand your old man would probably throw me out on my butt if you did, but I said, "That's all right. It's getting pretty late, anyhow, and I'd better be getting home." Then she turned and put her arms up around my God-damn neck and said, "Here's a kiss for the hero, anyhow," and that's when I found out for sure what I'd been suspecting already, that this little old Marsha was a real worker, and that it didn't make any God-damn difference which side of town you were on when you got down to business, it was the same wherever you were, only a little better some places than others, depending on who you were doing business with. I don't mind telling you that kiss would have blistered the paint on a new automobile, and she may have been pretty good at it and all that, but no doll is that good naturally, and the only way she gets that good is by a hell of a lot of experience. I sneaked in a feel or two upstairs, and she didn't seem to mind, but pretty soon she pulled away and skipped up the driveway laughing and said over her shoulder, "Goodnight, Skimmer. See you at school." I watched her go up between the big columns on the porch and through the door, and then I turned and started shank's mare for home, and as you can see, there hadn't really been much to it, just a kiss and a couple of feels where they didn't count much, and that's the way she worked on me.

I went on home and to bed, and I lay there listening to the old man snoring like a hog in the next room, and I thought, Hell's fire and save matches, was old Bugs right! Was old Bugs ever right! Then I began to think that one thing was sure as hellfire, that I couldn't be running around with my God-damn pockets empty if I was going to get anywhere with a classy doll like Marsha Davis, and what the hell would have happened if I hadn't been able to jockey old Tizzy into picking up the check at Tompkins', and I tried like hell to think of some way to pick up some easy dough, but I couldn't think of any, except shooting rotation at Beegie's, and I didn't have time for Beegie's any more, now that I was on the basketball team, and besides, rotation at Beegie's was just for crummy nickels that wouldn't get you to first base with a classy doll whose old man was president of a bank unless you had a God-damn barrel of them.

The next day at school everyone kept coming up to me and slapping me on the back and saying things like, "Boy, what a game, Scaggs! Man, were you hot!" and a lot of other crap like that, and it wasn't bad at first, being different from anything that had ever happened to me at school before, but after a while it got to giving me a pain and that's no lie. I kept on looking out for Marsha, but I didn't see her at all until school was almost over in the afternoon, and then it was in the hall with a lot of jerks between us, and she just waved and yelled, "Hi, Skimmer," over their heads, and that's all there was to it. I went to practice feeling pretty sore, and I thought more than once that just as soon as basketball season was over I was going to poke old buller Mulloy right in his fat mouth. Jesus, that guy was a pain. He was a pain up to here if I ever saw one.

Well, as it turned out I didn't see Marsha at school again that week, and I got to thinking it was just a God-damn one-night stand, and not much of a stand at that, and I told myself that I was a damn fool, anyhow, to think a snotty bitch like her would have any time for a guy like me who came from the wrong side of town and didn't have a cent but then I got to thinking abbut that kiss under the tree by the drive, and it sure as hell didn't seem like the kind of kiss a girl would give a guy if she didn't figure on having some time for him afterward, but of course some girls will kiss anyone who's handy, and that's just a cheap way to get their kicks. I got to thinking to hell with her, she wasn't the only pebble on the lousy beach, and to hell with basketball, the God-damn crazy game, you ran your guts out and threw a damn silly ball around for no damn reason except so a lot of clowns could jump up and down and yell fifteen rahs for this and that, and I was going to turn in my suit at the end of the week, and the last thing I was going to do was poke old Mulloy in the mouth and slap the b'jeesus out of Tizzy Davis. Then, would you believe it, on Friday, the day I was going to do it, old Tizzy came up to me in the locker room and said, "Oh, by the way, Scaggs, Marsha told me to tell you that she had to go out of town with Mother for a few days, in case you might wonder where she was, and I forgot all about it until right now." He said it just like that, the skinny bastard, just as calm and cool as a God-damn prince or something, and the worst part was, it changed everything again, and I couldn't afford to hit him.

So I didn't quit the team, and we made a trip out of town for a game the next night, which was Saturday, and we won the game, and I made twenty-six points. We rode on a bus that the school chartered, and we got back to town after midnight, and the next afternoon I went uptown to Beegie's and shot rotation, which was the first time I'd done it for a long time. When I got back home, the old lady was having a can of beer at the kitchen table, and she said, "Someone called you on the telephone," and I said, "Who the hell you mean, someone?"

"A girl," she said, and I said, "What girl?"

"How would I know what girl?" she said.

"God damn it to hell, didn't you even ask who she was?" I said.

"Why the hell should I ask her who she was?" she said. "She didn't want to talk to me."

"What the hell makes you so God-damn ignorant?" I said. "Anyone knows you're supposed to ask anyone's name when they call on the damn telephone."

Then she began to blubber and say that I wouldn't talk to my old mother that way if only Eddie was here, and I said that was a lot of bull and she knew it, and even if Eddie hadn't got killed in the war he probably wouldn't be around, any-how, because he'd probably be in jail, and that tore it for sure, and she began to bawl and howl about what a terrible sin it was for me to talk that way about my poor dead brother, so I got the hell out of there. I walked up the street a few blocks to a crummy neighborhood drug store and screwed up my courage and called Marsha, and sure enough, it had been her on the phone, just like I'd suspected.

She said, "Is that you, Skimmer?" and I said it was, and she said, "I just called you this afternoon."

I said, "I thought maybe it was you. That's why I called back," and she said, "Did you miss me around school?" and I said, "Well, I sort of looked around for you, but you didn't seem to be there," and then she let out this little squeal and

26

asked me if Tizzy hadn't told me what she'd told him to tell me, and I said he'd forgot all about it until Friday, and she said, "Oh, that damn Tizzy! I'll fix him!" and I thought, I hope she fixes you good, you son of a bitch.

"Well," she said, "I've simply had a deadly time all week. You know how it is when you have to go somewhere with your mother."

I said sure, I knew, but I didn't, as a matter of fact, because my old lady never went anywhere, and even if she'd run all over the God-damn place, she wouldn't have taken me with her. Anyhow, Marsha kept going on about how deadly it had been, and how she simply had to have something interesting and exciting to do or she'd go right out of her mind, and after a while it turned out that what she wanted with me was, she could have her old man's car for a couple of hours and would I like to take a ride? I said I didn't mind, which was the God-damnedest understatement of the year, and she said she'd drive by and pick me up if I'd give her my address, and I said it just happened I was calling from a drug store and she could pick me up there, and I gave her the address of the drug store and hung up.

I had fifteen lousy cents in my pocket, and I wondered what the hell I'd do if Marsha wanted to stop somewhere for a coke or something, and I was thinking that maybe I could get away with that old dodge of putting your hand in your pocket and feeling around and saying, "Well, Jesus Christ, what could've happened to the money I had? Do you suppose I could've left it in my other pants?" but just then who do you think I saw but old Bugs dropping a nickel in a pin ball machine at the end of the soda fountain. There was an outside chance that Bugs might have some dough, even if it was a damn slim one, so I went up to him and said, "Hi, Bugs, old boy. You happen to have an extra buck on you?" and to tell the truth, I never had any God-damn idea he had anything like that much, if any at all except the nickel he'd just dropped in the machine, but I could tell right away by the sneaky look that got on his face that he really had it.

"Hi, Skimmer," he said. "Where the hell would I get that kind of dough?"

"Same place you always get it," I said. "Out of your grandmother's purse."

27

It was a pretty good shot, and it was plain enough from the way old Bugs got all red in the face that I'd hit it right on the nose. Old Bugs had this grandmother who was about a million years old and got a pension from the government because Bugs's grandfather had been in some God-damn war back in the Middle Ages or sometime. Every month after she got her pension, she'd put part of it in the bank and put the rest of it in this little black purse she carried around with her. The way she carried the purse, she'd wrap it in a handkerchief and pin it to her long underwear under about six inches of other under-clothes and stuff, and the only way Bugs could get to it was to wait until she'd undressed and gone to bed. She kept pieces of hoarhound candy in the purse with the money, and you could always tell when old Bugs had swiped some money from his grandmother because it always smelled like this God-damn hoarhound.

Well, he swore up and down that he didn't have any, but I knew he was a damn liar and just didn't want to come across for a buddy, so I said, "Look, Bugs, don't give me any crap now, because I've got to have some lousy dough, and I'll tell you why. I got this date with Marsha Davis, and I'm stony, and she's going to be here any minute to pick me up in her old man's car."

He looked at me and said, "Oh, bull, you haven't any more got a date with Marsha Davis than I have," and I said, "The hell I haven't. You just stand up inside the window and see if she doesn't pick me up, and if you'll let me have a buck I'll tell you what I'll do. I'll try to fix you up with one of Marsha's friends."

That was a God-damn laugh, because no classy doll was going to have any time for old Bugs, even if he'd played on a dozen lousy basketball teams, and besides he was only a stink-ing substitute who hardly ever got to play in a real game, but it worked just the same, Bugs being pretty God-damn stupid when you got right down to it, and he said, "No bull, Skim-mer? You really think you could fix me up?"

I said sure, it was a cinch, and he forked over a buck, and sure enough, it smelled just like this stinking hoarhound. I took the money and started for the door, and Bugs followed me up past the soda fountain saying, "Don't forget now, Skimmer.

You promised to fix me up," and I said, "Sure, sure, I'll fix it, Bugs," even though I didn't really have any idea of doing any such damn thing, and I went on outside and stood by the curb and waited. It was quite a while before she got there, and I began to think how maybe she wasn't coming after all, and how old Bugs would hoot if she didn't, and how I'd knock his God-damn teeth out if he did, and that's for damn sure the trouble with having a classy doll like Marsha on the string, she always keeps your lousy guts in an uproar. Pretty soon she came, though, in this black Buick about a mile long. She pulled up to the curb and said, "Hop in, Skimmer," and I hopped in beside her and looked back through the window of the drug store, and there was old Bugs with his teeth hanging out, and I could see that he was just about to wet his drawers, he was so God-damn jealous.

We went buzzing along in this big Buick that was like riding on the damn air, it took the bumps in the crummy street so easy, and Marsha said, "Sorry I was so long picking you up, Skimmer, but Dad always has to go through this deadly routine of giving me simply *hours* of instructions when I take the car out, and it's just too sickening for words." and I said, "I was just fooling around killing time anyhow. Would you like to go over to Tompkins' for something?" and she said, "No, I don't think I'd better go to Tompkins', because I'm supposed to be over at Marion's, and if I went to Tompkins', Dad would be sure to hear of it. Honestly, I think that man has paid spies or something, and besides I only have the car for an hour, instead of two hours like I thought, and I know we can find something better to do than sit around in Tompkins' with a lot of juveniles. Honestly, Skimmer, don't you sometimes find them just too juvenile?"

I said I sure as hell did, and by that time we'd got out to the edge of town, not on a highway but on a little farm-to-market road, and she said, "What are you sitting way over on that side of the seat for, Skimmer?" Well, I may be a little slow on the uptake sometimes, but I don't have to be kicked in the teeth before I get the God-damn point, so I eased across the seat until I was right up against her, and she said, "You wouldn't bother me if you put your arm around me," so I did.

We kept on going out the gravel road until we got to the

river, and we kept talking about how she'd missed me, and I'd missed her, and how the past week had been longer than a damn year, and how strange it was how something had just gone bang like a God-damn bomb the minute we first looked at each other, and when we got to the river she turned off at the end of the bridge onto another little road that went along the bank down past some cabins. Pretty soon we came to one that was bigger than the rest, set in under some trees, and she stopped the Buick beside the cabin and said, "This is the old man's shack, in case you're interested. He comes out here fishing in the summers, and sometimes he brings his friends out here when they want to have a brawl that might corrupt their dear children if they had it at home. Isn't it just too disgusting how transparent fathers are?" I said sure, fathers were for the book, and I could have backed that up with some stories about my old man that would probably have made her think hers was practically a plaster saint or something, but I didn't and she slipped out of the seat on her side and said, "Let's walk down and look at the river."

We walked down to the bank and looked at the river going past, and she said, "There's something about a river that makes you feel kind of sad, isn't there?" and I said it made me feel that way too, which was a lie, and to tell the truth, it wasn't much of a river, and just a lot of God-damn muddy water as far as I could see. We kissed once while we were standing there, but it was too damn cold with the wind blowing at us across the river, and so we went back to the Buick and really got started. Man, we really wallowed all over the lousy seat, and I won't tell you what all we did, any details or anything like that, but it'll give you an idea when you hear what she finally said. She laughed this little laugh and said, "Tough luck, Skimmer. I'm in the saddle."

To tell the truth, it sort of got me for a minute, hearing her come right out with it like that, just as cool as a God-damn cucumber, because girls usually act like it was a stinking crime or something and will go all out to keep a guy from finding out anything like that ever happens, and once I razzed old Mopsy about it a little, and she got all colors and began to bawl like I'd accused her of being queer at least. Anyhow, that put a ceiling on us, but we kept fooling around a long time under the ceiling, and she kept whispering things to me like how cute I was, and rugged, and sort of tough-like and different from all the other guys she knew, and then she sat up all of a sudden and looked at her wrist watch and said, "Oh, my God, my hour's up, and we haven't even *started* home. My father will simply be livid."

Well, she took the Buick back up that gravel road like a bat out of hell, and I thought more than once that she was going to smash the damn thing up and kill us both, but to tell the truth, I didn't much give a damn. When we got back to town, she asked me where I wanted her to drop me, and I remembered that I still had old Bugs's dollar to spend, so I said, "Oh, just drop me off uptown somewhere. I think I'll loaf around a little." She let me off right in front of her old man's bank, which seemed sort of ironic or some damn thing like that, and just before she pulled away she turned and said as if it was just something she happened to remember at the last second, "Oh, by the way, Skimmer, a bunch of us are having a little party at the Club after the game Saturday night, and I wondered if you'd like to go with me."

"What club?" I said, not that it made any difference, because I intended to go, whatever damn club it was, and she looked surprised and said, "Why, the Country Club, of course," like what the hell other club is there?

"Oh, sure, the Country Club," I said. "I thought maybe you meant some kind of special club or something. Anyhow, I'd be glad to go."

She said swell, and she'd meet me outside the locker room after the game, and then she drove away, and I wanted some cigarettes, so I walked down to Dummke's to get them. Old Gravy was sitting on a high stool behind the counter reading the Sunday funny papers, and he looked up at me when I came in and said, "Well, well, if it isn't the God-damn hero. Getting his name on the sports page and everything."

I said, "Just cut the crap and give me a pack of gaspers," and he looked shocked as hell and made a big red O with his stinking mouth and said, "Don't tell me a big athlete like you smokes cigarettes," and I said, "Ha, ha, you think you're pretty God-damn funny, don't you?"

Usually you could needle the greasy bastard into blowing his

31

lid right away, but this time he didn't get mad at all, but just laughed and tossed the gaspers across the counter and said, "You know, that basketball racket's got possibilities. You get good enough, you might be able to make a big thing out of it for yourself."

I thought about old Marsha and me in the front seat of the Buick, and I said, "Maybe I've already made a big thing out of it," and his little eyes got all narrow and still all of a sudden, and he said, "What the hell you mean?" and I said, "That's none of your damn business."

Then he laughed again and gave me the change from Bugs's dollar and said, "Well, I read in the sports page how you made thirty points your first game and twenty-six your second game, so you must be pretty good. After you get a little sharper, you come around and see me, and maybe I can do a good thing for you, and you can do a good thing for me at the same time," and I said, "I wouldn't put you out if you were on fire," and went out.

I still had seventy-seven cents to spend, and I thought about going around to Beegie's again, but I decided not to go because there was a chance of running into old Bugs there, and besides, to tell the truth, I didn't get much of a bang out of Beegie's any more, so what I did was go to a diner for a hamburger and bottle of coke and then to a movie. It was a corny movie, and this doll who was supposed to be such hot stuff wasn't half as good as Marsha, and Marsha had got more done in the front seat of the Buick for free than this one did in a dozen fancy joints with rich guys all over the place offering her diamonds and fur coats and all kinds of stuff for it. After the movie I went home and started thinking about how I could get hold of some dough for the party Saturday night, because you'd sure as hell have to have a pocketful to go to the damn County Club, and I had exactly seven cents left out of Bugs's crummy dollar.

That week old Mulloy really worked the hell out of us, and he kept talking about what a tough game it was coming up on Saturday, and how we'd have to be a hell of a lot better than we'd been yet to win this one, because this team was really a sharp one that could beat half the colleges in the country, and altogether he laid it on so God-damn thick you knew it was a pack of damn lies and just a trick to scare us into working all the harder. Old Tizzy and I were getting our business down better all the time, and we got so we could tell by the blink of an eyelash just which way the other one was going to jump, and old Mulloy puffed and blew about what a classy combination he'd made out of us, just like it was all due to nothing but his crummy coaching, and the truth is, whatever caused it, we were slicker than grease.

Along about Tuesday evening I was walking home late, and I was still trying to think of a way to get my hands on at least a fin for Saturday, and who should I meet over on my own side of town but old Mopsy on her way home from the grocery store. I hadn't seen her to talk to since that night when her old man and old lady had gone to the movies, and she said, "Hi, Skimmer. How come you haven't been around to see me lately?"

I had a good reason, of course, namely that you don't eat hash when you've got roast beef, but I tried to make it easy on her and said, "Oh, I've been pretty busy with basketball and all," and she said, "You're really getting to be a big star, and I'm proud of you," and I said, "Well I guess I've just got a knack for it," which, like I've said before, was the way it was.

We kept walking along, and pretty soon she said, "How would you like to come over to my house Saturday night after the game? We could pop some popcorn and listen to music and have some fun."

"Your old man and old lady going to be home?" I said, and she said they were, and I said, "Then how the hell we going to have any fun?"

She said, "You oughtn't to say things like that, Skimmer. You sound like you never thought about anything else," and I said, "Is there something else to think about?" and she said, "Do you want to come, or don't you?" and I said, "No, as a matter of fact I don't, because I've got a date to take Marsha Davis to a party at the Country Club."

You could see it knocked her for a loop, me just tossing it off that way, and she got sulky and said, "I guess now that you're a basketball star and running around with someone like Marsha Davis, you won't have any more time for me," and I said, "I guess maybe I won't."

"Well," she said, "you don't need to think I care," and I said, "I don't give a damn whether you care or not, and besides,

33

you ought to be glad I don't come because you're so damn determined to save it, and if I was hanging around you might be tempted to spend it."

That really fixed things up swell, that made everything just fine, and at the next corner she turned and went over a block just to get away from me, and damned if she didn't go home and tell her old man what I'd said, just like she'd told on old Bugs when he tried to sneak a feel. The first I knew about it was when I got home the next evening, which was Wednesday. The old man was in the living room when I got there, and he said, "What the hell's this I hear about you talking filthy to Mopsy Beacon?"

He sort of took me off guard, to tell the truth, and my damn tongue wouldn't work right, and all I could say was, "Filthy? What the hell you mean, filthy? Who says I been talking filthy?"

"You know damn well what I mean," he said, "and you know damn well who says so. Mopsy's old man says so, that's who, so don't bother to tell any damn lies about it, and I can tell you I'm getting damn tired of having someone like old man Beacon jump me every time I turn around about some damn dirty thing you've been up to."

"That's just a crying God-damn shame about you," I said. "Besides, old Mopsy's just got her nose hard because I won't have anything to do with her any more, and all I told her was that if she was so damn anxious to save it, I'd just stay away and not tempt her to spend it," and the old man got quiet then and looked at me and said, "You mean that's really all you said to her?" and I said yes, and he said, "Well, that don't sound so God-damn filthy to me."

That set the old lady off, and she said to the old man, "That's right. Support him in his wickedness. How the hell can you expect him to be anything but a bum with no respect for womanhood when you say it's not filthy to say something like that to a nice girl like Mopsy?" and the old man said, "Who the hell asked you to horn in, and how the hell do you know who's a nice girl and who's not? You never had any experience at it."

The old lady began to bawl and cuss the old man and threaten to leave him for talking to his own wife like she was no more than a street-walker, and the old man said any time

34

she wanted to leave he'd be glad to help her pack, and they got going so good that they forgot all about me and Mopsy and how the whole thing had started, and I went in the kitchen and had some cold supper and left. I was still trying to figure out a way to get hold of a fin, because here it was Wednesday already and Saturday would be the day I'd have to have it, and I even thought about going uptown and trying to find a drunk to roll in an alley, but that's sucker stuff, that's really taking a big chance for peanuts, and I'd never done anything like that before, and I didn't do it now. I finally went over to Bugs's house and told him how I was working on that classy doll for him, and how I thought I might get the job done if only I could scrape up a fin for this brawl at the Country Club, and then I asked him if he thought his grandmother would be good for that much. He said, Jesus, no, it was a long time from last pension day, almost the end of the month, and he'd already got to his grandmother for all she could stand, so I said sure, thanks for nothing, and went away.

Walking along, I got to thinking, What if all of a sudden I'd just see a fin lying on the sidewalk in front of me, just see it lying there as big and green as a God-damn corn field, and I actually got to thinking about it so hard I got the idea that maybe I could make it happen just by thinking of it that way, so I closed my eyes and walked along a way with them closed, and then I opened them and looked down at the sidewalk, but there wasn't any fin there, of course, and nothing like that ever happens except in some God-damn corny story where some jerk finds some money, a nickel or something, and runs it into a fortune and then spends the rest of his life telling other people what a hell of a guy he is and what bums they are for not doing the same thing.

Just to show you how things go sometimes, though, I finally got the fin with hardly any trouble at all, and that was because Thursday was the old man's payday, and he got drunk at the tavern on the way home from work and passed out on the sofa in the living room in his clothes. As luck would have it, the old lady had gone over next door for a few minutes just before he came home, and I helped myself to a fin from his stinking pocket while he was flopped on the sofa, and that's all there was to it. He was a pretty shrewd old bastard, though, and

35

the next morning he missed the fin and accused the old lady of taking it. She said he was a damn liar, of course, which he was, and then she looked at me and said, "Wasn't you home when your old man came in?" and I said, "Don't go accusing me of swiping the God-damn lousy fin," and she looked back at the old man and said, "You lost it, you drunken bum. What the hell you want to accuse us of stealing your money for?" You could see the old man wasn't convinced of it, but there was always the chance it was true, so he let the matter drop and probably took the fin out of the grocery money later.

That afternoon at practice, we didn't do anything but take turns shooting free-throws and tossing the ball around and stuff like that because we never went at it very hard the last practice before a game, and afterward we all went in the locker room and sat around on the God-damn hard benches while old Mulloy drew diagrams of plays and stuff on a blackboard with a piece of chalk. To tell the truth, I couldn't see much sense to it, because once we got in a game we hardly ever used any of the plays but just ran like hell and banged the damn ball at the bucket, but I guess it made old Mulloy feel important to go through all that bull just the same. He'd be talking along about something, and all of a sudden he'd point his damn finger at someone like he was ready to pull the trigger, and he'd say real fast, "What would you do in these circumstances?" and then he'd go on to tell the circumstances, and whoever he'd pointed at had damn well better know what he was supposed to do or else get chewed. You could see from the way the bastard acted that it made him feel important as all hell, a real hot-shot coach and all that, but like I said, we hardly ever went in for any of that fancy crap in a game, and what's more, he didn't seem to give a damn whether we did or not, and all he'd do then was jump up and down on the God-damn bench and yell, "Run, run, run!" until you wanted to poke him right in his stinking mouth.

After he finished with the chalk-talk, which was what he called it, he started in with the old pepper crap, and that was even worse. The idea was to get us all steamed up over the game and ready to go out and give our all for the dear old school and such bull, and he began by telling us what a tough team this was we were going to play, and how we'd have to play like we'd never played before if we hoped to beat them, and at first he hadn't had much hope, to tell the truth, but now he was sorry as hell he'd had so little faith, and he wasn't ashamed to admit it and say right out he was sorry, and he knew we weren't going to hold it against him, or let him down, and he wasn't going to say anything more about it, not a God-damn word, but he knew we were going out there tomorrow night and win this game, and all in all it was just about the sloppiest crap you could ever hope to hear.

When it was all over and he let us go, I went over to old Tizzy Davis, because there was something that had been bothering me, and I wanted him to put me straight, but I hardly knew how to bring it up. I'd thought about it some and had decided that it would be best to be just sort of casual, so I said, "By the way, Tizzy, about this thing at the Club tomorrow night. I forgot to ask Marsha what the guys generally wear," and he said, "Oh, these things are just little informal brawls. Most of us just wear something like what we ordinarily wear to school," and so that was all right, a big relief, as a matter of fact, and if he'd said anything else I'd have been right up that old creek without a paddle.

I fooled around the house almost all day Saturday and started out for the school about two hours before time for the game to start, and the old man was home at the time and said, "Where the hell you off to now?"

"I'm off to school to play basketball, if you want to know, that's where I'm off to," I said, and he said, "I thought I told you to quit that God-damn foolishness," and I said, "Who the hell pays any attention to what you say?"

"I'll damn well show you who *better* pay some attention to what I say," he said, "and I'll tell you something else right now. You get home here early tonight and don't go lousing around Beegie's pool hall or bumming the streets, and I don't want any other old bastard like old Beacon telling me you been talking filthy or doing some other God-damn thing to shame your family."

I laughed right in his fat face and said, "Shame my family! If that's not a belly laugh I never heard one. What the hell could I do that would shame this lousy family? Just tell me what I could do, and what's more, I probably won't be home

37

until one or two o'clock, or maybe even three, because I'm going to a party at the Country Club."

He looked at me and said, "Don't be trying to impress me with any of your God-damn lies, because I know you're a damn liar and wouldn't tell the truth if you were getting paid for it by the hour," and I said, "Who the hell's trying to impress you? I don't give enough of a damn about what you think to even bother thinking up a lie for you, and if you don't believe I'm going to the Country Club, it's all right with me, and you can go to hell as far as I'm concerned."

He kept on looking at me, and I could tell he was beginning to believe I was telling the truth, and then he began to laugh sort of soft with his big sloppy beer-belly shaking up and down, and he said, "Well, damn! Ain't he getting to be a big-shot, though! A regular God-damn plutocrat, going to the Country Club and everything!"

He kept on laughing that way, like he thought it was a hell of a good joke on the other people who went to the Country Club, which maybe it was, come to think of it, and I turned and started to leave again, but he stopped me before I could get out the door, and he'd quit laughing all of a sudden. "By the way," he said, "where the hell you getting the money to go to the Country Club?" and his eyes were narrow and pretty mean, and I could see that he was remembering the fin that had disappeared from his stinking pocket, so I said in a hurry, "Who the hell needs money? You so God-damn ignorant you don't know that a guest of someone whose old man is a member doesn't have to pay for anything? I'm going with Marsha Davis, and no one has to pay for anything because her old man's a member."

Well, that part about my going with Marsha Davis really broke off in him, and he sat there gawking at me with his nasty mouth hanging open, and I got out before he could close it and start in on me again. I walked across town to the high school, and all the rest of the team were already in the locker room when I got there, because I'd lost so much time jawing with the old man, and old Mulloy was pacing up and down like a God-damn cat on hot rocks.

I got into my suit and sat down on a bench, and outside in the gym you could hear all the maniacs raising hell and giving

38

fifteen rahs for this and that, and the band was playing these snappy marches that make you lose what little God-damn sense you might have had to start with, and it got into you a little, at that, even though you knew you were a creep for letting it and should have had your tail kicked up between your shoulders. Just before time to go out on the floor, old Mulloy got out in the middle of the locker room and raised his arms like some evangelist or something who was trying to get everyone to pay attention, and when we were quiet he still didn't say anything but just stood there with his shoulders sort of stooped a little like he was tired as hell, and the silence kept stretching on and on until you wanted to jump up and yell at him, for Christ's sake, and then finally he said in this low, tired voice, "Fellows, this is where I get off. I've done my best for you, I've taught you all I know, and now it's all up to you. All I'm going to say is, I know you're going to get out there and give me all you've got." Then he turned and walked off to his crummy little office in this God-damn awful silence that was like a damn funeral or something, and his shoulders were stooped this way that seemed to say that it was all pretty damn hopeless, and he walked like every step damn near broke his back, but he wasn't fooling me any, and I knew it was just a corny act that was supposed to get us all juiced up and ready to run our guts out just to show him we could beat this other team, and probably he'd read about some big college coach doing it sometime or other, because, as a matter of fact, I don't think he had the brains to think of it all by himself. I'm bound to say it worked with the rest of the team, though, the God-damn spooks, and when old Mulloy was gone they all jumped up and started banging each other around, including me, and saying, "Let's go, gang! That's the old pepper, gang! Let's show Coach we can do it! Let's get this one for old Coach!" and I thought, Horse manure! I'll get it for old Skimmer, that's who I'll get it for.

Pretty soon we ran out on the floor in a line behind old Tizzy, who was captain, and the second we showed up everyone began to jump up and down and raise the God-damn roof, and the band broke into the school march that was really some college song they'd swiped and just changed the words some, and the guys and dolls in white pants and white skirts ran back and forth waving their arms, the dolls flashing their butts, and

39

we began running in for setups and passing the ball around and doing the things we were supposed to do to get warmed up. After a while everyone got off the floor except the referees and the two starting teams, and the game got started, and I'll tell you one thing, however full of bull old Mulloy was about practically everything else, he was sure right about that damn team being sharp as hell and hard to beat, and to tell the truth, I thought for quite a while we weren't going to do it. They were really tall, in the first place, a bunch of God-damn goons, and in the second place, they played firehouse basketball, just like we did, and they could run like wolves, and it's a fact that they were leading us by three points at the damn half.

Well, you can bet old Mulloy had forgotten all about his corny act by that time, and in the locker room he was so damn mad he was slobbering at the mouth and really chewed the hell out of us.

He said we weren't doing anything right, and the other team was making monkeys out of us, and as a matter of fact we were playing like a bunch of stumble bums who'd never seen a basketball before, but this was bull, too, and the truth is, we were playing a damn good game, but the other team was playing just as good and in fact, so far, three points better. We went back out on the floor for the second half, and it's a good thing we went when we did because I was on the verge of telling old Mulloy he could play the rest of the God-damn game himself if he thought we were such bums, and it just happened that we got the ball right away and banged it into old Tizzy, and Tizzy banged it out to me, and I jumped and pushed just as one of the guys on the other team hit me like a freight train, the dirty bastard, but the ball went through the hoop anyhow. This gave me a free-throw besides the bucket, and I made it, and we were all even. Old Mulloy over on the bench started yelling, "Go, go, go!" and that big mouth of his was just like a diesel horn, and the crowd picked it up and started yelling, "Go, go, go!" like a God-damn chant or something, and we went. For a while it got into you in spite of yourself, and you kept going like you'd sure as hell be shot at sunrise at least if you didn't, but then it began to get pretty damn thin, and you just wanted to sit down on the lousy floor and let all the loud-mouths come down and go themselves for a while and see how they liked it, the sons of bitches. By that time, though, we'd run those goons down to where they were about two inches high and had built up a ten-point lead, and we never lost it, and I was high point man again with twenty-seven points.

In the locker room was the same old bull again, everyone horseplaying and slapping tails and old Mulloy strutting back and forth and gobbling like a God-damn turkey. He'd changed his tune again, now that the game was won, and he said he'd never doubted for a minute that we'd win it and that this little old team wasn't going to lose a game all season, and as a matter of fact it was true, and that's the way it turned out, but I've got my own opinion about how much he had to do with it. I'll say one thing, though, and that is, I'm damn glad we *did* win all our games, and I'd sure as hell hate to play on a team coached by that bastard that *didn't* win, because all this stuff he was full of about clean play and sportsmanship was a lot of bull, and all he wanted us to do was win, and he started getting mean as a damn alley cat every time it looked for a while like we might not do it.

I was just about dressed when old Tizzy came over and said, "I've got the old man's car, Scaggs, and you and Marsha are supposed to ride out to the Club with Marion and me. You about ready to go?" I said I was and hurried up and finished dressing, and Tizzy and I walked out in the hall together, and Marsha and Marion were waiting there. Marsha grabbed me by the arm in that way she had and began telling me what a great game it was, and how wonderful I'd been, and how she was just simply limp from excitement, and I thought, Well, Skimmer, it looks like a big night, and as a matter of fact it was.

Marsha and I rode out to the Country Club in the back seat, of course, and old Marion was sitting all plastered up against Tizzy in front, and he was driving the damn car with one hand all the time and didn't have any time to pay any attention to what Marsha and I were doing in back, and we were doing plenty and then some, and the truth is, in spite of Tizzy and Marion being all tied up in their own business, I was a little worried about the damn rear-view mirror. It didn't take long to get to the Club, not near long enough from the way I looked at it, and we drove up this long gravel drive in front of the clubhouse, and we all got out and went inside

41

but Tizzy, and he drove the Buick on down to park it and come in afterward. The clubhouse was built on a slope, and there was a big front veranda on the ground floor, and we went downstairs to the room where we were going to have the brawl, and it was still on the ground floor there, too, only on the back because of the slope, and there were big glass doors that opened onto another veranda that looked right out over the golf course. The doors were closed, naturally, because it was cold, but you could look out over the course that was smooth and rolling with trees scattered around over it, and the moon was up out there, about as big as a God-damn washtub and a kind of orange color, and it wasn't too bad if you didn't have any more to do than look at it.

There were a lot of other guys and girls there that I'd seen around school, and we went through the great game, Scaggs, routine, which was all right to loosen me up and make me feel at home, because to tell the truth, I felt like a slob right at first and mad as hell because I did, and if anyone had said the wrong thing, I'd probably have clobbered him right in the mouth. No one said anything wrong, though, and someone started a stack of platters going on a big phonograph against the wall, and Marsha and I started to dance, with her all up and down the front of me, and after that it was free going, with me loose as ashes all the way.

In the next room, which was the bar, there was a bunch of old crumbs having a party, and I guess they were really supposed to be looking after us, but as it turned out, before it was over, they needed someone to look after them. They were drinking highballs and stuff like that, and we were drinking cokes, and after a while a couple of guys in our bunch slipped in and swiped a bottle of whisky from behind the bar and brought it back, and we spiked up some cokes and passed them around, and everything was going pretty good until one doll got sick and checked her cookies in the middle of the floor, and that tore it. Three or four old guys came in from the bar next door and took away what was left of the spiked cokes and probably drank them themselves, the bastards, and I was ready to throw them right back where they came from on their tails if I could've got anyone to pitch in, but I couldn't. After that, someone cleaned up the mess, and an old doll who had about three sheets in the wind and was doing her damnedest to hide it came in and said in this God-damn coy voice that fun was fun and no one wanted to spoil it but just to think about what we did before we did it, and Marsha looked at me and said in this voice that she made sound just like the old doll's, "Well, I've already thought about what I want to do next, so let's go outside and do it."

Well, some guys may need an engraved invitation, but not old Skimmer, so we slipped out through the glass doors and across the veranda and started down across the golf course, and Marsha said, "Have you ever played golf?" and I said I hadn't, and the truth is, I hadn't thought much about it at all, except that there didn't seem to be any God-damn sense in it whatever, and I've heard my old man say that anybody who'd carry a bag of clubs around for miles hitting a little ball in front of him must have damn little to do and be queer in the head besides. Anyhow, old Marsha didn't really care whether I played or not, or even answered her question, and neither did I, for that matter, because we both had something else on our minds that even my old man could see some sense in now and then. We went quite a way across the grass to a big tree and sat down under the tree and began to kiss and fool around, but the wind whipped in under the tree, and it was cold as hell, and before long I could hear her teeth rattling together and feel little goose pimples all over her skin.

"I'll tell you what," she said. "Let's go find the car," and to tell the truth, I was ready to go almost anywhere myself to get out of that damn wind, and under the circumstances, that probably gives you a pretty good idea just how damn cold it was. We went back across the grass at an angle to the parking lot and down a row of cars until we came to the Buick, and Marsha said, "This is it," and I started to open the door, but damned if old Tizzy hadn't locked it, the skinny bastard.

Marsha stamped her foot and said, "Oh, that damn Tizzy!" and I said, "What the hell would he want to do a thing like that for?" and she said, "Oh, that's just like him, he doesn't give a damn about anyone else as long as he's got the keys to get in himself in case he gets that drippy Marion to come outside."

Anyhow, the cars on both sides kept the wind off of us, and

43

we stood there and did a lot more kissing and fooling around, and it wasn't so bad after all, but not as good as it might have been, and Marsha said we'd been gone so long someone might miss us and we'd better go back, and so we did, but no one had missed us at all, and we might as well have stayed outside all the rest of the time we were there as far as I could see, except that it was pretty damn cold.

As a matter of fact, though, we finally got on a sofa out in another little room that was almost as good as outside, besides being warmer, the only trouble being that you had to be sort of careful and not do too much and be ready to pretend that you were just sitting there talking if anyone else came in. Marsha kept telling me how I was just what she'd always wanted, the strong type that always knew just what he was after and wasn't like all these other guys that seemed so juvenile, and I said she was just what I'd always wanted, too, and she said she knew there wasn't anything on earth that could keep us apart, now that we'd found each other, and altogether it was damn good stuff, in spite of being largely bull, and it didn't seem like any time at all before one of the old dolls from the bar came in and said we had to get the hell out of there and go home.

It was about midnight then, but we didn't go home but went to an owl diner in town instead and had sandwiches and stuff to drink and listened to the juke box. When it got time to leave, I decided I'd better pick up the check, because if I kept letting old Tizzy do it someone might get the idea I was a God-damn deadbeat, or something, so I did, and old Tizzy said I didn't have to do it and let him pay half at least, but he didn't insist very hard, damn him, and it cost me a dollar and twenty-eight cents with tax. We got in the Buick again and started off, and old Tizzy saying, "Well, now, how shall we work this?" and I knew what he was getting around to was, should he take me home first or Marsha, and the idea was that, either way, he didn't want us around to cramp his style when he took Marion home.

If there'd been any way to louse him up, I'd have done it, just for locking the door of the God-damn Buick, but there wasn't any way that I could see, so I said, "Why don't you just let me off at your house with Marsha and then I'll walk on home," and he said, "Oh, you don't want to walk clear across town this time of night," and I said, "Sure I do, I like to walk," and so he said well, have it your own way, which I intended to, and he drove up to his house and let us out in the driveway.

I walked Marsha up to the front steps, and we stood there in the dark and kissed and fooled around some more, quite a bit as a matter of fact, and she said, "I wish I never had to go in," and I said I wished she didn't either, and she looked up through her lashes and gave this little laugh and said, "Better yet, I wish you could come in and stay all night," and I said I sure as hell wished I could, too, but that it would be a damn hot day in January before we ever got her old man to see it the same way. She said that was right and fathers were a hell of a problem when you came right down to it, and then we loved each other up pretty good for the road, because she was getting shivery and goose pimply again, like on the golf course, and so was I, to tell the truth, and besides, old Tizzy would be getting back any minute and it was time she was getting in.

I went home to bed, and I lay there thinking about what a hell of a big difference this God-damn crazy game of basketball had made in everything, and how the difference might even have been a little bigger by this time if only the weather had been warmer, but there was always another time coming up, and I began to get the idea that maybe I had something really big by the tail, a hell of a lot bigger than old Bugs or I had ever thought, and God only knew what might come of it if I really kept at it and worked it for all it was worth. I was just about to go to sleep when I remembered the change from the fin that was still in my pants pocket, and I got up and got it and stuck it in the toe of my shoe, because it would've been just like the old man to sneak in and go through my pockets to see if I'd really taken the fin and had anything left, the sneaky son of a bitch.

Well, if you were around at the time and read the sports page, you'll remember that I went through with this basketball stuff, just like I decided to, and really made a big thing of it. I got my picture in a lot of papers in other towns, even, and stories about how I was the best damn sharpshooter anyone had ever heard of, and I guess I must have been, at that, because I was high point man in the league all season and wound

45

up after it was all over being high point man in the whole God-damn state. In the league, every team had to play each other twice, home and home, which means once on each other's court, and old Mulloy really sweat out the game we had to play on their court with the team that damn near beat us on ours, and he was a genuine pain in the tail, the way he kept pointing us for that particular game, as he called it, and trying to juice us up with his corny crap that was supposed to be psychology or something.

It turned out that he did all his sweating for nothing, anyhow, because we beat them on their own court easier than we had on ours, and from then on we just coasted in and were league champions going away. I kept going out with Marsha all this time, and I'm not going to say a hell of a lot more about it, except that she was a real classy doll who always knew just what the score was, and that the weather wasn't always as God-damn cold as it was the night we had the party at the Country Club.

After all the leagues in the state had finished playing and had a champion, they divided the state into regions, and all the champions in each region played each other in what was called regional tournaments. It happened that it was the year to have our particular regional tournament in our own gym, and that was a break for us because a team usually can do a little better on its home court, and the school really made a God-damn production of it. We had these big pep rallies in the auditorium, with the cheer leaders and the band there and everyone going crazy, and old Mulloy was really in hog heaven, and you'd have thought to hear him talk that the bastard had won the championship all by himself. Every day on the sports page of the paper there was a big black headline that said ALL THE WAY, FELLOWS, and when we finally got around to playing the games, it seemed like everyone in town except my old man and old lady tried to get in the God-damn gym, and I'm bound to say that it got out of hand and pretty God-damn silly, all in all, but it was all gravy for Skimmer any way you looked at it, and who the hell was I to complain?

Anyhow, to make it short, we went through the tournament like a dose of salts and were regional champions as well as league champions, and I was voted most valuable player by the God-damn coaches, and that didn't leave anything but the state tournament, where all the regional champions played each other, to wind it up. The school had a big outdoor rally to send us off, and they had these crazy God-damn snake dances through the streets and a hell of a big bonfire on a vacant lot uptown, and old Mulloy made a stinking speech about how wonderful it was to have such support and how no team can get anywhere without everyone behind them and urging them on to victory, and it wound up with an old wooden building catching on fire, and it looked for a while like they were going to burn down the whole God-damn town.

After a while I got tired of it and looked around for old Bugs to walk home with, but I couldn't find him, and then I decided I'd walk around to Dummke's and get a package of cigarettes before I went, because we were leaving on the bus the next morning for the town where the tournament was going to be played—you probably remember it was a town called Stockton—and I figured I might not have a chance to buy any afterward. When I got to Dummke's, it was someone besides Gravy behind the counter, and he gave me the gaspers without any lip, and the two cents change from the two-bits I gave him, and I was on my way out the door when Gravy came out of the back room and said, "Hey, kid, what's the hurry?"

That struck me as pretty God-damn fishy right away, because always before I couldn't be in a big enough hurry to suit him, but I just stopped and looked at him and said, "Who the hell's in a hurry? I got my God-damn cigarettes, and I'm leaving, that's all," and he showed all these stinking white teeth all over his greasy face and said, "Don't be like that, kid," and I said, "Like what?" and he said, "Always with a God-damn chip on your shoulder. Why in hell don't you relax once in a while? How'd you like a coke on the house?"

If I'd had any doubt about him being up to something, I sure as hell didn't have any after I heard him say that, because any time Gravy Dummke gave anything away, even a lousy coke, you could be damn sure he was looking at it as an investment of some kind, but to tell the truth, I was curious to know what it was he had on his crummy mind, and besides, I didn't have any objection to the coke, either.

"Well, thanks all to hell," I said. "A whole God-damn nickel coke? You sure you can afford it?"

His fat face smoothed out the way it did when he was about

47

to flip his lid, and his little eyes got mean for a second, but then he found his teeth again and shrugged and said, "Always kidding. Damned if you ain't the greatest God-damn kid for a joke I ever saw," and I went back, and he got a bottle of coke out of this crummy cooler he had at the end of the counter and took the cap off and handed it to me. I lit a cigarette and started drinking the coke, and he said, "Ain't it against the rules for guys on the basketball team to smoke?" and I said, "Screw the rules. Besides, what the hell business is it of yours?"

"None," he said, "but I'd hate to see the star of the team kicked off the night before the state tournament started," and I said, "That's a laugh. That God-damn Mulloy wouldn't kick you off for murder if he thought it might make him lose a game," and he laughed and said, "Well, you're safe, then, because I guess they wouldn't have much chance without you," and I said they sure as hell wouldn't, and he said, "That leaves you in a pretty good position, kid, you know that?" and I said, "What the hell is that supposed to mean?" and he said, "Why don't you come on in the back room and talk it over. I hate to see a smart kid not taking advantage of his opportunities," and to tell the truth, I thought it was just some of Gravy's nonsense, but then I thought it wouldn't cost me anything to listen at least, so I went.

The back room was a crummy dump a little bigger than an outdoor privy with a dirty window looking out on the alley and a few tables and chairs scattered around where the God-damn penny-ante bastards that hung around Gravy's could play pinochle and poker and different card games, and there was no one there but Gravy and me. He told me to take a load off my feet, which I did, and he sat down in another chair across the table from where I sat, and he asked me if I wanted another lousy coke, and I said I didn't, and he said, "Jesus, kid, you're really getting to be somebody. Every time I look at a God-damn sports page there's your name or picture or something, and to tell the truth, I never dreamed all the time you been coming in here for cigarettes that you'd be such a big shot basketball player."

I hadn't dreamed it myself, as a matter of fact, but I wasn't telling him that, so I said, "You can just skip the crap, Gravy. You didn't ask me to come back here just so you could pin a

48

medal on me," and he laughed again and said, "You're a pretty smart kid. That's one thing I always knew, even if I didn't know you were going to be a big star and everything, because I can smell a smart kid a mile away," and I said, "So I'm a God-damn marvel or something," and he said, "Not quite. Not yet, anyhow. Even a smart kid's got to learn the ropes. For instance, I bet you don't know just how big this basketball thing can be. A lot of money changes hands on basketball games, kid, even high school games," and I said, "Well, if you've been riding our God-damn team, you ought to have a potful," and he looked at me for quite a while with his face smooth and his nasty little eyes half asleep, and then he said, "Oh, I've been getting *my* share. Have you been getting *yours?*"

I thought about how everything had changed after I'd started playing the God-damn crazy game, about Marsha and going places I'd never gone before and everyone thinking I was a regular ring-tailed wonder, and I said, "I've been doing all right," and he said, "Oh, sure, a few stinking kids setting you up to cokes and hamburgers and a few girls flipping their tails in your face because they think you're a lousy hero, but I'm talking about the long green, kid, the folding stuff, the stuff that counts. How much of that you been getting?"

I said, "You know damn well they don't pay you anything for playing basketball at school," and he said, "Sure, I know it, but that wouldn't keep a smart kid from taking care of himself," and I said, "You give me a pain in the ass, if you want to know it, because you're always acting like a big shot and blowing about all the lousy money you got, but as far as I can see you're just a small town jerk running a cigar store, and I never saw you with more than a fin in your hand in my life."

I stood up then and was going to get the hell out of there, but he dug down in his stinking pocket and pulled out a wad of bills that would've choked a mule, and he peeled off five of them and laid them on the table, and they were all tens, and I stood there looking at them.

"What's that for?" I said, and he said, "It could be for you, and maybe another hundred later," and I said, "What's the angle?" and he said, "You want to sit down and listen, I'll tell you. No charge for listening," and I figured there wasn't, so I sat down.

He got out a cigarette and lit it and rolled it around in his stinking fat lips until it was soaked about half an inch down with his nasty slobber, and all the time he kept looking at me through the smoke like he'd probably seen some big shot do in the movies or something, and pretty soon he said, "That team of yours could go all the way in this state tournament," and I said it sure as hell could, and he looked at me some more and said, "As long as you're playing, that is," and I said that was sure as hell right and I was sure as hell going to be playing.

He laughed and threw his cigarette into a can half full of water on the floor, and the cigarette went out with a little hiss. "Well," he said, "that's up to you, and probably you'll get fifteen rahs and a couple of cokes for your effort, but I was thinking if you played all the games but the last one you might make a good thing of it," and I said, "How good?" and he said, "Like I mentioned, this fifty now and a hundred later," and I said, "That's all right, but I don't like the idea of looking like a God-damn monkey by getting beat in the finals. I got my reputation to think of," and he said, "You're a smart kid with brains, so why the hell don't you use them? You won't look like any monkey, but just the opposite, because you'll get sick and not be able to play at all, and everyone will say just see what happens when old Scaggs isn't in there. The first game old Scaggs doesn't play, the God-damn crummy team loses," and when I came to think of it, I knew it was true and that's just what everyone would think.

"I don't know," I said. "It'll look pretty fishy, me getting sick that way at the last minute," and he said, "Hell, kid, everyone's got the right to get sick. It would be too big a chance to have you throw it on the floor, because, besides hurting your reputation, you're too God-damn green to get away with it without making it stink to the rafters. Remember, though, you'd have to get sick right at the last minute, in the locker room or something, because otherwise the news would get out and change the odds, and if you lose before the finals the whole thing's off, but you can keep the fifty for your trouble."

I sat there and thought about it, and it sounded pretty good, not only the one-fifty but the idea of everyone saying that stuff about see what happens when old Scaggs isn't in there, and I got a bang just thinking about old Mulloy tearing out what little

50

hair he had left and beating his God-damn chest, the son of a bitch, and it was almost as good as poking him in the mouth. After a while I stood up and took the five tens off the table and put them in my pocket, and it was the most money I'd ever had at one time, and you could see it was just like pulling five of Gravy's God-damn back teeth, and he said sort of slow, "Remember, kid. Don't try any tricks. I got ways of handling. smart bastards who try to cross me," and I said, "You just have the God-damn hundred ready, that's all, and don't bother trying to scare me with any crummy threats because in my opinion you're just a fat slob with a big mouth."

I went home then and put the fifty in my shoe and went to bed, and I thought that the returns from this basketball stuff were sure picking up and that it was a God-damn shame it was so close to being all over, and that was the first time I really began to wonder if there wasn't some way I could go on with it.

The next morning I got up and got ready to go to Stockton for the tournament, and when I went out in the kitchen for breakfast, the old man was sitting at the table and the old lady was frying his egg at the stove. The old man stood up and bowed like he'd met a God-damn king or something, and he said in this snotty voice, "Well, well,. if the God-damn hero ain't honoring us with his presence. It's damn generous of you to come out and sit down with common folks," and I said, "Ha, ha, you kill me. You're about as funny as a lousy crutch," and he said, "What with being a God-damn hero and having your name and picture in the paper and running around with a bank president's daughter, I don't suppose you'll be having much of anything more to do with your old man and your old lady," and I said, "What the hell's the matter with you? What the hell you want to start this bull first thing in the morning for?" and the old lady spoke up at the stove and said, "Just the same, I notice you haven't brought your fine girl friend around to see your old folks," and I said, "You think I've lost my marbles or something? Why the hell would I want to louse everything up by bringing her to this lousy dump with you and the old man raising hell all over the place?"

The old man said, "Well, maybe we ain't good enough for you any more, but I notice you're around regular enough when your God-damn belly's empty," and I said, "As far as I'm concerned you can take your God-damn slop and feed it to the hogs," and then he started around the table after me, so I got the hell out of there and walked uptown and had breakfast at a diner, using one of the tens I'd got from Gravy Dummke to pay for it, and when I got to the school, the bus was parked out front with a big crowd around it and the band playing, and there was a hell of a big banner fastened on the bus that said, ALL THE WAY, FELLOWS, just like it had been saying in the paper.

Well, when I walked up there was a big God-damn cheer and everyone started yelling, "Scaggs, Scaggs, Scaggs!" and there was a guy with a camera there from the paper, and he took my picture, and Marsha was there, too, and she wanted to get in the act just like these damn girls always do, which was all right with me, and she put her arms around me and gave me this big kiss that must have lasted a whole damn minute at least, and damned if the guy from the paper didn't take a picture of that, too, and it came out in the paper that evening with some big black printing under it that said, A WARRIOR'S FAREWELL. I got on the bus then, and everyone razzed me about the kiss and said pukey things like, "Oh, you dog!" and "How do you do it, Casanova?" whoever the hell he was, which I got the idea he must have been hell with the women, and old Mulloy pranced up and down the aisle and said, "The old pepper, fellows, the old pepper," until you wanted to tell him to sit down, for Christ's sake, and shut up, and the truth is, the crazy bastards kept it up all the way to Stockton, which was damn near a hundred miles, and it's a wonder the driver didn't run the God-damn bus in the ditch and kill us all.

We had three rooms in a hotel in Stockton, and I was in a room with Tizzy Davis and another guy and old Mulloy himself, which was a God-damn lousy break if I ever had one, because he was one of these sloppy bastards who sing in the bathtub and slop water all over the place and leave their God-damn crappy shaving stuff thrown all over, and every time you turned around or wanted to sneak a cigarette or something, there the son of a bitch was. Besides, he kept going on and on all the God-damn time about what we'd have to

52

do to win the tournament, and what we'd have to watch out for when we played this team or that one, but how he knew we could do it and nothing was going to stop us now that we'd got this far, and I couldn't help thinking that all the other teams had got this far, too, and probably felt the same way about it, and altogether he was such a pain in the ass that I got to thinking again about how he was going to feel after the last game, and I had a hell of a good time thinking about it.

After we were settled, he got us all together in our room and delivered a God-damn lecture about athletes being gentlemen and not destroying private property, meaning the hotel, and I could tell from the way he said it that he'd had some pretty bad experiences with things like that, and he went on to tell us we had become famous and had acquired a moral obligation to set fine examples for all the kids who admired the hell out of us, and he wasn't going to snoop or anything but was going to put us on our honor and have perfect faith in our integrity and trustworthiness and crap like that. Then he wound up saying, "Now, fellows, on to the state championship! The old pepper, the old spirit!" and everyone jumped up and yelled and beat on each other, and Tizzy Davis said, "Three cheers for Coach," the brown-nose creep, and they gave the cheers, and a couple of guys got old Mulloy up on their shoulders and started to march around the room with him, but the fat bastard was too heavy, and they dropped him, and it sounded like he was going right through the floor, and as a matter of fact it looked to me like they'd started to tear up the God-damn hotel already.

Well, we played our first game that evening, and we won going away, and there's not a hell of a lot of use going into it any more than that, or any of the other games in our bracket, either, except to say that we won all of them, and I was high man in every damn one, and we had to play Stockton in the finals, because they won all the games in their bracket, too. They were pretty good, all right, and they had this guy who played center and was about as tall as a God-damn building and was practically a freak, as a matter of fact, and old Mulloy was in a regular sweat about it, because he knew this guy would be all over old Tizzy like a dirty shirt, and old Tizzy wouldn't be able to hook any shots over his head, and it looked like it was going to be all up to me outside the keyhole. I didn't tell him that I had what was left of fifty bucks in my pocket that said I wasn't going to be there, and I had it all figured about pretending to get sick, just how I was going to do it, and the evening of the game we were all lying down in our rooms resting, which was something old Mulloy made us do, and when he came in, saying, "All right, fellows, time to go, this is it, the old pepper," I got off the bed and started to sway a little and hold my head, and he said, "What's the matter, Skimmer," and I said, "Nothing. I'll be all right. I just felt a little dizzy for a second, that's all."

He grabbed me by the arm and held me up like I was a lousy drunk or something, and he said, "Here, now, fellow, you can't go getting sick on us just before the big game," and I said, "I'll be all right, don't worry," and he said, "Well, I hope so, for your sake as well as the team's. I wasn't going to tell you about it, because I thought it might make you nervous and throw you off your game, but as a matter of fact there's a scout down here from Pipskill University just to watch you play this game, and if you're sharp he'll probably offer you a big athletic scholarship or something. I've known for a long time they had their eyes on you, and this is it, fellow, this is the one that will make or break you."

I said, "What's an athletic scholarship?" and he said, "Well, they pay all your expenses at the University and give you a job besides that isn't much of a job, and they set you up in a swell frat house, and all this is just so you can play basketball on the Pipskill University team," and I looked at him and started thinking about it and said, "No bull?" and he said, "That's straight stuff, Skimmer, and what's more, there are always a few loyal alumni around with a lot of money and the good of the school at heart, and they're always making little donations to the star players and things like that."

What I had in mind was to pull that little act about being dizzy in the hotel room just to soften them up so it would seem more like the real thing when I pulled the big act in the locker room later, but now I kept on thinking about this Pipskill University stuff that old Mulloy told me, and I'd never thought about going off to college or very much about going on with basketball, but now I could see how I could do it, and I knew all of a sudden that I was *going* to do it, and to put it plain, I wound up thinking, Well, screw Gravy Dummke. It's every man for himself.

"I'm okay now," I said. "You don't have to worry about me," and it was the truth. Old Mulloy slapped me on the shoulder and said, "That's the spirit, that's the old fight," and we got all the other guys and went out to the school and suited up and waited a while for the end of the consolation game, which was the game between the two teams for third and fourth places, and then we went out on the floor and warmed up, and I knew just what I was after and was as cool as a God-damn cucumber.

Just as soon as the game started, it was pretty damn plain that old Mulloy had been right in sweating this one, and old Tizzy was in for a bad night, because this God-damn goon who played center on the other team was all over him all the damn time, and he hardly ever got a chance to hook one over and had to pass out to me. Old Tizzy's poison was my meat, though, because I got a hell of a lot more shots this way and more chances to look sharp for the scout, and as a matter of fact I was feeling good and hotter than a pistol, and damned if I didn't wind up with forty points in the game, and in case you don't know it, that's a hell of a lot of points. The other team was hot, too, though, the bastards, and every time I made a bucket, it seemed like they went right down and made one themselves, and my forty points plus what the other guys could scratch out now and then were damn near not enough, and the truth is, we were ahead by the skin of our teeth, one point to be exact, when the game ended. Anyhow, we were state champions, and the school got a big cup, and the guys on the team all got little medals that were cheap as hell, to tell the truth, and I got a little cup of my own, besides, for being voted most valuable player again by the God-damn coaches.

In the locker room old Mulloy went clear off the deep end, as nutty as a peach orchard bore, and he kept running around to all us guys and saying, "Hi, champ. How's it going, champ?" but all I could think about was that lousy scout from Pipskill University, and kept wondering where the hell he was, and I got the idea old Mulloy had been feeding me a line just to juice me up, which would've been just like one of his God-damn crazy ideas, and I thought, I'll champ you, you son of a

55

bitch, if there wasn't really a scout like you said. When I was dressed, though, and had just about given up, in came this guy about six and a half feet tall and shook hands with old Mulloy and said, "Congratulations, Elroy," which turned out to be Mulloy's first name, for Christ's sake, and Mulloy brought the guy over and said, "Skimmer, this is Mr. Dilky, the man from Pipskill U that I was telling you about." This guy Dilky reached down and shook my hand and said, "Well, Skimmer, that was a great game. I guess you must be pretty hungry after that, aren't you?" and I said I was, and he said, "Suppose you and I just run downtown to a restaurant and have a steak and a little talk," and I said that was okay with me.

We went out and got in his car, which was no less than a God-damn Caddy, and drove downtown to this fancy restaurant and had steak dinners that cost him three bucks per, because I got a look at the check, and while we were eating he said, "Well, Skimmer, I understand this is your last year in high," and I said it was, and he said, "Have you considered attending Pipskill U?" and I lied and said I had but that Pipskill was pretty expensive and I didn't know if I could cut it down there, and he said, "Well, I'm not going to beat around the bush, Skimmer, and I'm here to tell you right now that you can come to Pipskill if you want to."

I said, "How's that?" and he said, "I was authorized by Barker Umplett, head basketball coach at Pipskill, to offer you an athletic scholarship if you looked good enough, and I don't mind telling you that you looked plenty good enough to me," and I said thanks, he didn't know how much it meant to me to hear him say it, which was true enough, but not in the way he thought, and then he explained to me how I'd get all expenses paid and a job that wouldn't take any of my time to speak of and a hundred dollars a month for doing the job. As a matter of fact, I hadn't dreamed I'd get that much, and I was damn sure ready to grab it, but just the same I thought it wouldn't do any harm to push my luck a little, so I said, "Well, that's fine, but my folks are pretty poor, and I don't have any money to buy clothes to go to college in and things like that," and he laughed and said, "Think nothing of it. Soon as I get back to Pipskill I'll send you something to take care of these incidentals. We have a little fund for that purpose," and that sewed it up, and we shook hands on it, and he drove me back to the hotel in the Caddy.

The next morning we went home in the bus, and there was a big celebration there that I'm not going to tell about, because it was just more of the same old crap, and I hung on at school till it was over, since it was only a couple of months, anyhow, and I kept going around with Marsha, and it was really something with the weather warmer, and I looked forward to it for the whole summer, but damned if she didn't go away on a vacation and not get back until damn near September, and by that time I was about ready to leave for Pipskill and had other things on my mind.

That's about all there is to it, how it started and how it grew, but I guess before I quit telling about the high school part and start telling about the Pipskill part I'd better tell how it came out between Gravy Dummke and me. As a matter of fact, nothing happened at all for a long time, not until after school was out, and you can bet I kept out of his God-damn cigar store, and I'd just about come to the conclusion that he'd decided to cut his losses and nothing was *ever* going to happen when all of a sudden it did. I went to town one night and shot rotation at Beegie's, and I was leaving to go home when this guy I'd never seen before said, "You going home, Scaggs? I happen to be going your way, and I'll give you a lift." He was a short guy, but pretty heavy, with one smeary eye that looked like a stinking broken egg and red hair and so God-damn many freckles it looked like the old cow had blown bran in his face, and he kept picking his nose, which is why I didn't suspect him of anything, I think, because who the hell suspects anything of a guy who picks his nose? I'd heard some of the guys in Beegie's call him Pinky, so I said, "Sure, Pinky, thanks," and we went out together and up the street to his car, which was a Chevvie. There was another guy sitting in the back seat, but I didn't even see him until this Pinky guy and I had got in the front seat and started off, and then I saw him, and I don't see how the hell I missed him in the first place, because he was as big as a God-damn barn.

We drove fast as hell down the street and around the corner, not toward the side of town where I lived, and I said, "Where the hell you going?" and Pinky said, "You'll find out," and

57

I said, "Well, I don't know where the hell *you're* going, but I know where *I'm* going, and that's home, so you can just stop this God-damn can and let me out," and he said, "You're a smart little bastard, aren't you? We don't like smart bastards. It's our job to teach smart bastards it doesn't pay to be so damn smart."

By that time I knew what was happening, that it was Gravy Dummke behind it, and I said, "So you two goons are doing the dirty for that fat slop Gravy Dummke," and Pinky said, "Who's Gravy Dummke? Never heard of him," and I said, "The hell you haven't, and you can tell him from me that someday I'll get his God-damn greasy hide for this," and then the big guy in back reached up and clobbered me behind the ear, and I couldn't say anything more or hear a damn thing but bells for at least five minutes, and when I'd got over it we were out of town on a gravel road and kept going down the road for about half a mile and stopped. I didn't figure there was any point in being a lousy hero with no one around to see it, so I jumped out and started to run, but I tripped in the God-damn ditch and fell on my face, and they were on top of me before I could get up, and the big guy had fists as hard as rock that must have weighed about twenty pounds apiece. They beat the hell out of me, I'll have to admit it, and as a matter of fact they damn near killed me. They'd drag me up on my feet and then take turns knocking me down again, and once I hauled off and kicked one of them in the crotch, and he fell down and held himself and rolled around yelling, but as luck would have it, it was the little one, and still left me with the big one. After a long time it just seemed to stop all of a sudden, and this was because I passed out, and when I came to, they were gone, and I was still in the ditch.

Well, it took a hell of a long time and was pretty tough going, but I finally got home to bed, and the next morning I was a mess and lied to the old man about being in a gang fight with a bunch of high school guys from another town, and it tickled the hell out of him, and he said it damn well served me right for being a bum. I never told anyone the truth about it all, but I made up my mind I'd get Gravy Dummke for having it done to me, the son of a bitch, and I finally did, too, and I'll tell about it later in the place it comes.

Part II: *PIPSKILL U.*

WELL, LIKE Marsha would have said, the summer got pretty
God-damn deadly before it was over, and I was glad to get
away from the old jerk town when September finally came.
I went up to Pipskill University, which was just outside the
city on a big hill beside the valley that a river went through,
and at first I felt sort of funny being away from everyone
I knew, and I wished someone had come up to school with
me, someone like old Bugs, or even Tizzy Davis, but Tizzy's
old man had sent him back east to some crummy college that
went in mainly for books instead of things like basketball, and
old Bugs was too God-damn dumb to go to any kind of
college whatever. That was the difference between Bugs and
me. I was pretty ignorant myself, I mean, never having taken
the trouble to crack any books except once in a great while,
but old Bugs was just plain dumb, and the difference between
us was the difference between being ignorant and just plain
dumb, which is quite a difference. A guy who's ignorant is a
guy who could learn if he wanted to take the trouble, but a
guy who's dumb is just S.O.L. when it comes to anything in
the brains department. I don't want to overdo this ignorance
stuff, though, as far as I was concerned. What I mean is, I was
ignorant about most of the crap you were supposed to know
from books when you got into a college, but I knew quite
a bit about a lot of other things.

Old Pipskill was a kind of pretty place, I'll have to admit
that, and you could sit up there on the hill where all the buildings were and look down into the valley where the river was,
and it wasn't half bad. Most of the buildings were made out of
this gray stone that you see around, and they all had this
God-damn green ivy crawling all over them, and there were
all these big trees around that spread out over the walks
you walked on, and here and there in various places there
were these cast iron statues of guys who had given something

59

or other to Pipskill, or had gone to school there and had later got to be big shots in some way, but I went around and looked at the names under all these statues, and I hadn't even heard of a one of them before, and I couldn't help wondering what the hell was the use of being a big shot in a way that hardly anyone ever heard of, and I made up my mind that if I ever got to be a big shot it would be in a way that got noised around.

The first thing I did when I got there was go around to the gym to see the basketball coach, whose name was Barker Umplett, like I told earlier, but the guy I saw was this guy Dilky who had scouted me out at the tournament, and it turned out that he was the freshman basketball coach as well as a scout. He'd gone to Pipskill himself once and had been a big basketball star who'd got his picture in *Collier's* and stuff, and in fact I learned that one magazine had printed a whole article about no one but him, and the reason I learned this was because he showed it to me just so I wouldn't have any doubts about what a wonderful bastard he was.

He was sitting in a stinking little office just off the locker room when I got there the first day, and he stood up and shook my hand in this God-damn manly way that damn near cracks your bones and said, "Well, well, Skimmer, I see you made it," and I said I had, and he said, "Well, how do you like old Pipskill U?" and I said what I'd seen of it looked okay, and he said, "The more you see of it, the better you'll like it," and I thought, Well, I'll make up my own God-damn mind about that, and then he took me out through the locker room and showed me the gym.

To tell the truth, I didn't think much of it, and it was pretty old and dark when the lights weren't on, and there wasn't much room for anyone to sit and watch, and as a matter of fact it didn't seem as good as the one in the high school. I was just about to say something about it looking like a God-damn crackerbox to me, but before I had a chance he said sort of off-hand, "This is just the old gym where the freshman team practices, of course," and I felt a little better and asked him where the hell the first team played, and he said, "Oh, they use the field house. Haven't you been down there yet?" I said I hadn't, and he said, "I'll take you down and show it to you right now. Man, it's a honey," and he did, and it was.

It was made out of gray stone, like the other buildings, only it was a lot newer and didn't have any ivy on it, and from the outside it looked like a great big God-damn cow barn, but on the inside it was fancy as hell and looked like it covered about a thousand square miles and had enough room for about a million people to sit and watch, and as a matter of fact old Dilky said there was room for fifteen thousand. I got to thinking that fifteen thousand people could make a hell of a lot of racket if they were even half as crazy as the God-damn spooks who went to the games at the high school, because there were usually only a couple thousand at the high school at the most, and I found out later that the people who watched the games at Pipskill were even crazier, and when you played in the field house it was just like being in all the God-damn nut houses in the world wrapped into one. As a matter of fact, Pipskill was what's called a basketball school, and no one cared if the stinking football team wound up in the cellar every year, which it always did, but if the basketball team didn't win the league championship and everything else that was around to be won, somebody better look out for his God-damn head.

I might as well say right now, though, that I didn't get to play much in the field house the first year because they had this lousy rule that you could only play three years on the first team—the varsity team, it's called—and the first year you had to play on the crummy freshman team, and you went around and played the freshman teams at the other schools in the league, and no one paid much attention to it. I was against the rule and thought it was pretty God-damn crummy, and I tried to think of a way to get around it, and I asked Dilky if I couldn't play the first three years and just skip the last one, but he said I couldn't and it was just something I'd have to put up with, though he thought himself that it was pretty stinking not to let a guy play four years.

After we'd looked at the field house, old Dilky took me around to the frat house where I was going to stay and introduced me to a guy named Mellon who was a senior in the school. This guy turned out to be the big cheese around the frat house, and I didn't like him from the start because he had this snotty attitude, and you could tell just by looking at him that his old man was loaded, a God-damn millionaire or something, and the truth is, he was nothing less than the vice-president of a railroad, as it turned out. Anyhow, this Mellon spook had a way of tipping up his chin and looking at you down the sides of his stinking nose, and his nose would sort of quiver like whoever he was looking at needed a God-damn bath, and he looked at me this way and held out a hand with the fingers kind of dangling from it. "How are you, Scaggs?" he said, and I said I was all right and took his hand, and it was just like picking up a handful of fishing worms, and he said, "I understand you're a damn fine basketball player," and I said I sure as hell was.

Old Dilky said, "Well, Skimmer, I'll leave you to get settled now. We don't start serious practice for another month, but you'd better drop in afternoons and start getting your eye back," and I said I would, and he went away, and Mellon said, "You'll be bunking with Spicer. Come along now, I'll show you your room." I didn't know who the hell Spicer was, but I followed Mellon upstairs to the room, and Spicer wasn't there, but it was a damn swell room, and I don't mind saying it was a hell of a lot better than any room I'd ever had or thought about having. Mellon hung around a few minutes telling me some of the God-damn house rules I was supposed to mind, but I didn't pay much attention, just wishing he'd go the hell away and leave me alone, and after a while he did, and I went over to the window and looked down at the yard.

It was a big yard with the grass as green and smooth as one of Beegie's pool tables and a box hedge all around it that was clipped slick and level on top by someone who knew just how to do it, and the house itself was a lot like the house Marsha lived in, only bigger, with white pillars at the front and green shutters at the windows and everything, and as a matter of fact I was damn lucky to get a fancy place like that to flop in, because usually you had to be pledged and voted in and all that crap, but they had it set up to let star basketball players in without it, and I'm not kidding myself a God-damn bit that I'd have never got in otherwise, but otherwise, as far as that goes, I wouldn't have been at the God-damn school at all.

I flopped on the bed and lay there thinking that this was sure as hell the life and wishing that the old man and the old lady could get a look at me now, and I was still lying there when the door opened and this guy about six feet tall came in, and he had sort of sandy hair that stuck up every which way on his God-damn head and a nose that looked like it had got caught in a knuckle shower, and he saw me flopped on the bed and said, "You're Scaggs, and I'm Spicer," just like that, just like he'd settled the God-damn issue once and for all, and it annoyed the hell out of me, to tell the truth, and I said, "The hell we are!" and he stopped and laughed and ran his hand through his crazy hair and said, "Well, aren't we?" and I was bound to say then that I was Scaggs, at any rate, and he could damn well be Spicer if he wanted too.

He sat down in a chair and swung his legs up over one arm and said, "I suppose old Bunny brought you up," and I said some creepy bastard named Mellon had done it, and he said, "That's Bunny," and I said, "Why the hell you call him Bunny?" and he said, "Didn't you notice the way his nose quivered? Like a damn rabbit's?" and I said I had, as a matter of fact, and he said, "Well, that's why we call him Bunny."

"He acted pretty snotty, if you ask me," I said, "and just between us I felt like poking him in the mouth," and he said, "Everyone feels like that about Bunny, but no one ever does it because he's got all the God-damn money in the world, or anyhow his old man has, which is the same thing in the long run. Personally, I think he's a fairy."

"What makes you think he's a fairy?" I said, and he said, "Well, he's got this damn dainty way about him, you just watch the way he flips around and goes on about things, and you never see him with any girls or anything, in spite of having a car of his own and all that money, and besides, he was kicked out of some school back east, and everyone thinks that was the reason, so don't let him get you in any dark corners."

I said it would be a sad day for fairies when the son of a bitch got *me* in a corner, and I asked him how long he'd been there, and he said a couple of days, and I said it seemed to me he knew a hell of a lot for a guy who'd only been around two days, and he said, "Oh, I pick up things fast," and then he looked at me for a long time like I was a stinking freak in a sideshow or something, and finally he said, "So you're another one of old Umplett's whores."

It made me a little hot, to tell the truth, and I said, "What the hell you mean, whores?"

"Basketball player," he said. "Like me."

"Where'd you get that whore stuff?" I said, and he said, "Oh, don't get your bowels in an uproar about it. I just call us that because of the way we get paid and kept and all, and I guess if I include myself you got no call to bitch, and besides, I'm all for it, and it looks like a hell of a good life."

Well, I had to admit that he had the right to call himself anything he damn well pleased, and if it just happened to include me, that was just tough, and what was more, when I got right down to it, I sort of liked the God-damn goofy bastard, and that's the truth of it. I asked him where he'd played basketball, and he said over in the next state, and he'd had a pretty good deal at the state university over there, but at the last minute old Dilky had shown up with a better one, so he'd changed his mind and come to Pipskill. I told him about how I'd been top scorer in the whole damn state and most valuable man in all the tournaments and everything like that, and he asked me what my points total had been, and I told him, and he whistled and said I must be pretty damn good at that and he'd bet we'd make what he called a damn good one-two punch on the Pipskill team, and all in all I had a feeling we were going to get along good together, and he started calling me Skimmer, and I started calling him Micky, which is what he said he wanted to be called.

The very next morning I got enrolled in some classes, and later I took a test that was supposed to show if you were bright, and I guess I was bright enough at least, because I never heard any more of it, and I got the general idea that they didn't much care how God-damn ignorant you were just as long as there was some chance they could teach you a little something later, and I'll have to admit there was another test I took that turned me up ignorant.

This was a test in spelling and grammar and how to say things the right way and all, and I guess I didn't do much on it, and as a matter of fact, from what they told me, hardly a damn thing. They gave you this test so they'd know which rhetoric class to put you in. Rhetoric is what they called it, but it was the same damn thing they called English in high school, only they made it a little tougher for you, and it had always given me a pain in the you know what, and it still did. Everyone had to take it, there wasn't any getting out of it, and they had it divided into three classes that they called Rhetoric I and Rhetoric II and Rhetoric Zero. Rhetoric II was for the God-damn geniuses or something, and Rhetoric I was watered down a little for the ones who were no better than they were supposed to be, and Rhetoric Zero was for the ones who loused up the test, and I was in Rhetoric Zero.

This class in Rhetoric Zero only had about ten guys and one girl in it, and the guy who taught it was about the spookiest guy you could hope to meet outside a freak show. He was tall and thin with bones that stuck out at all his God-damn corners, and he had this long face with sad eyes that made him look like a mule, and when he walked his arms and legs just flew off in any damn direction they pleased without any relation at all to the direction he was supposed to be going, and honest to God, it looked like he was about to fly all apart any damn second.

The first day of the class he walked in like this, and he put his crummy old beat-up brief case on the desk and stood there looking at each one of us in his turn without saying anything, and then after a while he said in this God-damn deep voice, "Maybe you're wondering why I'm teaching this class instead of someone else, and I must tell you now that it's in punishment for my sins, and how bad those sins are I'll leave you to surmise from the degree of the punishment." Well, even a guy in Rhetoric Zero knows when he's being called a God-damn boob, and I didn't like it, and I'd have clobbered the bastard if he'd ever said it again, but he didn't. As a matter of fact, though, what he did was worse, but it wasn't anything you could clobber him for and explain it afterward.

What he did, he'd talk to you like he was reading out of a primer to a kid, and when you didn't know something about the damn crummy rhetoric that you were supposed to know, he'd just look at you with these mournful eyes that were like a mule's and let out this long sigh and say, "Now, Mr. Scaggs, let's go over it once more," and he'd bear down on the Mr. like it was a God-damn honorary title or something. His name

65

was Boxer, and I don't mind admitting I got to hating the son of a bitch, and the longer I was in the class the more I hated him, and I finally got to hating him even more than I hated Gravy Dummke, in spite of the fact that Gravy hired two guys to beat the hell out of me. What made it worse, I just couldn't put my mind to that rhetoric bull, and I never seemed to know any answers to what he asked me. They had a whole God-damn file of questions and answers on most subjects at the frat house, and generally these got me by pretty well in the other classes I took, but nothing seemed to do any good in rhetoric.

Meantime, I went back to the gym and saw old Dilky again and asked him about my job. He looked down at me with a blank look on his face like maybe I'd asked him who was the second king of Peru or some God-damn place like that, and he said, "What job?" and I said, "The job I'm supposed to do for the hundred clams a month I'm supposed to get," and for a minute, the way he looked, I began think it had been a lot of bull he'd fed me just to get me up to Pipskill and that there wasn't really any job or any hundred clams a month, but then he laughed and said, "Oh, *that* job. Well, we'll think of something after a while, maybe. Right now, you just come in and sharpen up your eye and don't worry about it."

"Well," I said, "it's not the God-damn job I'm worried about, it's the hundred clams," and he laughed again and said, "Oh, you'll get the hundred, all right, regular as clockwork the first of every month," and sure enough, the first of the next month I got the hundred, and I got it on the nose every month after that, too, but old Dilky never got around to thinking up a job for me to do to earn it, which was all right with me, if that was the way he wanted it, and I damn sure wasn't going to make any issue of it. I kept going in every afternoon to sharpen my eye and get in condition, and there were some other first year guys who came in, too, including old Micky Spicer, and old Dilky got to making us run around and around the God-damn gym for our wind and our legs, and as a matter of fact it wasn't much fun, but mostly a lot of work, and after a while I began to figure that I was earning my lousy century and then some.

There was one guy who came in whose name was Carboy,

and this guy was damn near seven feet tall and still growing, and Barker Umplett, the head coach, had snaked him in off the prairie somewhere to play center for him. He was pretty good in lots of ways and got around on the floor pretty good in spite of being so damn tall and awkward, and he was great stuff for reaching up and snatching rebounds off the board, which is pretty damn important in itself because it keeps the other team from getting more than one shot at the bucket at a time and helps you to keep on shooting yourself until you finally hit it, but the worst thing about him was that he couldn't hit a bull with a spade. It damn near drove old Dilky nuts. He worked with this Carboy all the time, trying to teach him how to hook over and hit the bucket, but when he hit one now and then it was mostly just an accident, and the truth is, you just couldn't tell where in hell the God-damn ball was going once he let loose of it. Honest to God, it might go sailing clear up over the lousy backboard or anywhere.

About the middle of October we really got into it in earnest, and I soon found out then that playing basketball in high school wasn't anything to playing it in college, even on a crummy freshman team, and this Dilky had been pretty easygoing up to then, but afterward he wasn't easygoing at all, and as a matter of fact old buller Mulloy had been a stinking piker by comparison. He didn't run up and down and yell, "Go, go, go!" all the time like old Mulloy, but he let you know pretty quick that he *expected* you to go, and if you didn't do it, or even let down a little once in a while, the slop really hit the fan, and once when old Carboy slowed down to about eighty miles an hour Dilky stopped the action and walked out on the floor and got the ball and stood there real quiet and polite and smiling at Carboy a little, and he said in this soft voice, "Run, Mr. Carboy, run, God-damn you." And then damned if he didn't haul off with the God-damn ball and knock old Carboy ass over elbows, all seven feet of him.

Every now and then, after we got started good, Barker Umplett would come over from the field house to watch us work, and he'd stand there and look us over and not say anything at all, and after a while he'd go away, and all in all he was about the creepiest bastard I ever saw, and maybe it's time I told you a little about him, but not much, because I

67

didn't see a hell of a lot of him that first year, him being busy with the first team over in the field house, and I can tell about him better when he comes in more.

He wasn't very tall, only about five feet seven or eight, but he was damn near as wide as he was tall, and he probably weighed around two hundred pounds without any flab to his belly like there'd been to old Mulloy's, and altogether he looked like he'd been hacked out of a chunk of rock. He had these bushy eyebrows and hair growing out of his God-damn nose and all over his chest like a bramble patch, and as a matter of fact he was about as hairy as a guy could get, except on his head where a guy usually wants a little hair, and on his head there wasn't any at all, not a God-damn spear, and it was just as naked as the palm of your hand. Under those bushy eyebrows that stuck out in all directions, his eyes were about the color of cold dishwater, and when you looked in them you were liable to get the impression that the bastard was blind, because they had this empty kind of look that blind guys have, and if you did get that impression, it was your God-damn mistake, and as a matter of fact he saw a hell of a lot more than you ever thought he did or wanted him to. He wasn't the old buddy-buddy type at all, like old Mulloy all the time and old Dilky some of the time, and all the years I played for him at Pipskill he never gave me a good word or a pat on the back, nor to anyone else, either. This was because of the way he looked at things, and I'll tell you later how it was he looked at them.

Well, everything kept going along pretty good and about as expected, the basketball team shaping up for a good season and the lousy football team losing all their God-damn games, and after a while it got to be close to Thanksgiving, and it was about then I got called in for a consultation with this spook Boxer I told you about, and I knew damn well in advance what it was for, because I'll have to admit things hadn't picked up any in the rhetoric class. He was sitting behind his desk when I got there, and this doll was sitting in another chair in front of the desk, and I didn't pay much attention to her at first, except to notice that she wore goggles that were pointed up at the corners where the handles fastened on and had little sets in them that were supposed to look like diamonds or something and were really glass.

Old Boxer looked at me like he was about to break out bawling from the general sadness of things, and he said in this fancy way he had, "Sit down, Mr. Scaggs. I know your time is infinitely precious, and I won't claim any more of it than is absolutely necessary," and I could tell he didn't mean it the way it sounded, but just the opposite, the snotty bastard, and I sat down and said, "I got all day," and he said, "Unfortunately, I haven't, so I'll come right to the point. I am aware, of course, that you are a shining, ascending star in the heavens of basketball enthusiasts, and this places me in a precarious position because you have demonstrated beyond doubt over a period of time that it is utterly futile to expect you to make a passing mark in Rhetoric Zero, and nothing sets a shining basketball star any quicker than a flunk in rhetoric, and nothing sets the star of a simple teacher in this school any quicker than setting one of the stars of Coach Umplett. If all this is making you see stars, Mr. Scaggs, you have my sympathy, because I'm seeing them, too, and it has indeed been my misfortune to see far too many of them for much too long."

That's about the way he said it, as near as I can put it down, and you could tell he thought it was clever as hell to break it off in me that way, but the truth is, he had me a little confused from trying to follow him, and before I could make up my mind to clobber him or at least say something back he went on. "In other words, Mr. Scaggs, as a man named Cellini once put it, my guts are in the sauce pan, and consequently, in order to salvage then, I'm prepared to compromise my integrity still another time, to sell another little bit of my soul. This young lady sitting here is Miss Sylvia Pruet. Miss Pruet has brains. Miss Pruet takes to rhetoric like a duck to water. Being myself too great a coward to undertake the odious task, I've prevailed upon Miss Pruet to tutor you. I'll insist upon calling it tutoring, even though I really know better, and I have no doubt in the world that it will be largely a matter of your simply turning in her work, because while I have utter faith in Miss Pruet's brains, I have none whatever in her ability to withstand the corruption of an ascending star. All I ask is that you support me in my pitiable delusion by disguising the work, by copying it in your own hand, and for Christ's sake, be certain to make plenty of errors short of failure, because any reasonably accurate paper from you would be evidence of cheating that even I couldn't ignore."

Well, I didn't know who the hell this guy Cellini was, and still don't for that matter, but I could tell easy enough when someone had spit in my eye, and I was about to tell him what he could do with his Miss Pruet, but then I thought what the hell was the use of fouling my own nest because of this spook, and I didn't tell him because I knew he was just the kind of unreasonable bastard who would really flunk me if I pushed him to it. I started thinking about the hundred clams a month and the soft life at the frat house with old Mickey and the other guys and all the other things that might develop from this God-damn game that I didn't even know about yet, so I finally stood up and said, "Well, it's all right with me, if it's all right with her," meaning this Pruet doll, and she stood up and said, "I'll be happy to help you all I can," and I looked at her good for the first time then, and I was glad I'd gone along with it after all, because to tell the truth, she wasn't a bad looking doll whatever. She wore these fancy goggles, like I said, but they didn't seem to hurt her much, and she had a lot of good stuff wrapped up in a sweater and skirt, and her face wouldn't have stopped any clocks, either, in spite of being kind of sappy and dewey in the way you'd expect in any doll who went in for rhetoric and literature and crap like that. Besides, to tell all of it, I had this thought that she ought to be a pushover for a guy like me who played basketball and got to live in a frat house without being voted in and everything like that, and as a matter of fact she was.

We went outside and started walking across the campus together, and she said, "When do you want to begin your lessons, Mr. Scaggs?" and I said, "Call me Skimmer," and she said, "Very well, you may call me Sylvia, then," and I said, "Sylvia's a pretty name. I always wanted to meet someone named Sylvia. You ever get a name in your mind and just go on for a long time wishing you could meet someone with that name?" which was a lot of bull, of course, because I'd never thought about meeting anyone named Sylvia and didn't even think it

70

was such a hot name at all, as a matter of fact, and I guess she didn't swallow too much of it, anyhow, because she just looked at me and said, "When do you want to begin your lessons, Skimmer?" and I said, "You're the teacher."

"Very well," she said. "I suggest that we meet three evenings a week and that you come over this evening to make a beginning," and I said, "Over where?" and she said, "Drayton Hall," which was a place the dolls lived who weren't in sororities and stuff, and I said, "What time?" and she said, "Around seven," and I said I'd be there.

We'd come along to the old gym by that time, and I had to go in, so I said, "I got to go in and practice basketball now, and as it is I'm late, and old Dilky will be blowing his stack," and she said, "Don't let me detain you," and it sounded pretty snotty the way she said it, and I made up my mind right then to have her talking out the other side of her God-damn face before I was through, and I said, "Well, I'll see you around seven," and she said, "Very well," and I found out later that she was always using that crummy expression, very well, and when she walked off I could see that her skirt fit pretty tight and had a nice wobble to it.

I practiced and went back to the frat and ate and got my God-damn rhetoric book and went over to Drayton Hall, which was a big stack they'd built with money that had been left to Pipskill by some old doll name of Drayton and was called Mother Drayton's Fun House by the guys at the frat and others. There was a desk in the hall with a doll behind it, and she said, "Whom are you calling for?" and I said, "Sylvia Pruet," and she said, "If you'll just have a seat in there, I'll call her," and what she meant by in there was a big room with sofas and chairs scattered around, and quite a few of the girls who lived there were doing this and that with guys who had come to see them, and I went in and sat, and pretty soon old Sylvia came down. She looked pretty damn slick, if you want to know it, and I got to thinking that what had looked like a damn dull year at Pipskill, what with having to play on the crummy freshman team and no one paying much attention or anything, might pick up after all and turn into something pretty good, and the truth is, I was damn glad I had trouble with the lousy rhetoric and needed a tutor.

71

"Well, Skimmer," she said, "shall we get started?" and I said that was what I'd come for, which might have been all of the truth in the beginning but wasn't any more by a damn sight, and we got on a sofa in one corner of the room and went at it, the rhetoric, that is, but to tell the truth I had something else on my mind and couldn't show much progress, and after about an hour I said, "I just can't seem to put my mind to it with all the noise and the people around and everything," and she said, "Perhaps you're right. I think we'd better use the library after this."

We arranged it between us to meet at the library three nights a week, and we did it for a couple of weeks, and studied, and I picked up a little on the rhetoric, but not much. It came around Thanksgiving then, and school closed up for a week, the classes, that is, and nearly everyone went home, but I didn't, and neither did Sylvia. We went on meeting at the library just like we'd been, only now it was every night instead of only three, and we had the room we studied in pretty much to ourselves, and to tell the truth, we started doing less studying and more other stuff, and I guess now's the time to tell it and get through with it.

She was nuts, this Sylvia Pruet was. All slobs who go for literature and stuff like that are nuts, of course, but she was even more nuts than most. She asked me if I liked poetry, and I said I didn't, except the kind of dirty limericks my brother Eddie used to teach me before he got himself killed, and she said it didn't do any good to talk to her that way, because she'd made up her mind that all my toughness and everything was just a kind of protective armor to keep me from being hurt and that I'd been hurt terribly sometime or other and had been embittered by it. This was strictly bull, but I could see it made me look romantic or something to her, so I didn't deny it, and she said she'd like to teach me to love poetry the way she did, because she knew I was the type would really go for it once I got into it, and it looked like an angle to me, so I told her she might be right and I'd try to learn if she thought there was anything in it for me.

After that we only spent about half the time on the rhetoric, and the other half she'd read this poetry to me, and it was enough to make you puke, honest to God. The poems she liked

72

best and read most were all full of Aprils and lost loves and broken hearts and all sorts of crap like that, and they were written by someone I'd never heard of, name of Sara Teasdale, and one night after we'd left the library we sat on a stone bench in the dark out behind the museum, and I was just about to make a pitch and see if she'd do a little business when she said, "Oh, the fall, Skimmer, the beautiful fall. I think fall is just the most perfect time, don't you?" and then before I could say yes or no she started reciting this poem by Sara Teasdale that was all about how someone named Robin had kissed her in the spring, and someone else named Strephon had kissed her in the fall, but how a third guy named Colin had only looked at her and hadn't kissed her at all, and personally I thought Robin and Strephon had showed some pretty good sense for guys in a poem but that Colin was altogether a simple bastard, and I said so.

She reached up and patted me on the cheek and said I was just hiding my tender emotions behind a false front and that the point was that the most powerful feelings were often mute and undemonstrated. To show how this was, she went on and finished the poem, which told how Robin's kiss was lost in jest and Strephon's in play but that Colin's, which had only been in his crummy eyes, kept right on haunting her and everything, and it was just more than I could stand, and I said I guessed it was pretty enough but awful dull. That tore it for the time, and she got up and walked off back to Drayton Hall and wouldn't say another word to me, and I got to thinking that maybe she wouldn't meet me at the library the next night, either, but I went there and waited when the time came, and she did.

She said hello, and I said hello, and she sat down and asked me if I wasn't sorry for the way I'd talked last night, and I wasn't in particular but said I was, anyhow, just to get things going again, and she said, "I don't feel like rhetoric tonight, Skimmer. Let's go for a walk," and this was fine with me because I didn't feel like rhetoric myself at the time, or any other time, either, for that matter, and so we went outside and walked along to the same bench behind the museum and sat down. We were sitting there not saying anything, but just looking off down the slope in the darkness, and all of a sudden I

73

began to recite this poem, and I'll admit I'd gone to the library and looked it up and memorized it just that afternoon, because I thought I might need it to get me in good again, and it was just a short one about how I'd once been as fresh as rainwater but was now as bitter as the God-damn sea.

When I got through it, she said, "Oh, Skimmer, I knew it, I knew it. I knew you were just all hurt and twisted up inside like a little boy," and she said it in this chokey voice, and I looked at her close, and damned if she wasn't really bawling. She was so damn intense and nutty about it altogether that I began to get a little uncomfortable, to tell the truth, and I was just thinking maybe I'd better get the hell out of it when she turned and threw her arms around me and kissed me about sixteen times. Well, that wasn't any time to be leaving, as you can see, so I started to give her as good as I got, and she kept saying things about how I was good and noble underneath and she'd known it all the time, and she was shaking and running her hands over me and things like that, and what she was, she was one of these dolls who ordinarily keep themselves all corked up tight, and then a guy comes along at the right time and just touches them and they blow the cork and fizz all over the place. We sort of got out of control and kept going from one thing to another, and the short of it is, I got to her there on the bench, and afterward she started to cry again and say over and over, "Say you love me, Skimmer, say you love me," and finally I had to say it to get her to shut up about it.

Well, I might as well tell all of it while I'm at it, and that wasn't the last time, one place or another, and mostly she acted pretty sensible about it, and I didn't think too much about it when it wasn't happening, but then one night when I was with her she said, "Skimmer, I'm worried," and I said, "What about," and she said, "I'm three days late," and I said, "Late for what," and she said, "Late, Skimmer. You know," and then I did all of a sudden, and it scared the hell out of me. I don't mind admitting I was in a sweat about it, and I got to thinking about a movie I'd seen about a guy who got a girl that way and took her out in a boat to drown her but lost his nerve and wasn't going to do it but then did it accidentally, anyhow. I wasn't really so damn dumb as to think of trying anything like that myself, but I was trying hard enough to think of some

74

other way out of it that wouldn't ruin everything, all that the basketball was bringing and everything, and then after I'd sweated myself into a God-damn blue funk, damned if she didn't show up one night a little later and say, "It's all right after all, Skimmer," and I'd had plenty by then and said, "The hell it is. It may be all right with you, but it's not all right with me, and I wouldn't touch you with a ten foot pole if I flunked a dozen God-damn rhetoric classes."

I didn't go for any more rhetoric lessons, and I worried about it some because I knew sure as hell that old Boxer would give me the ax, but then something happened that just shows you how these things work out, and there just isn't any damn use worrying about them at all. I was telling old Micky Spicer about Sylvia one night in the room at the frat house, about how nutty she was and everything, and he said, "What the hell were you studying rhetoric with her for," and I said, "Why the hell *would* I be doing it? Because I was flunking the damn course, naturally," and he said, "You mean you're having trouble with that stuff? Man, it's duck soup," and I said, "It may be duck soup to you, but it's not duck soup to me, and if you're so God-damn good at it, maybe you can give me a lift," and he said, "Sure. Why not?" and damned if he wasn't as good as he claimed, and after that he always did my work for me in no time.

I didn't see old Sylvia any more, except now and then at a distance on the campus, having quit the rhetoric lessons, and just to show you how nutty she really was, she started letting herself go to hell like one of these dames carrying a torch in a corny movie, and there just wasn't any damn sense in it whatever that I could see. Mainly it was just the way she looked, the way she drooped around and had shadows under her eyes and acted like there wasn't anyone else in the lousy world, and about a month after I broke off the lessons she went away from Pipskill and didn't come back, and I learned later that she'd had a nervous breakdown and been sent to a rest home, which is just another way of saying she'd flipped her lid and been packed off to a fancy booby hatch. Another thing I learned, I learned that she'd had these nervous breakdowns before and was the kind of doll who'd go along all right for a while until some damn little thing triggered her off, and then

75

she'd go through one of these nutty periods until she finally came out of it again, and I thought it was about the dirtiest damn trick I'd ever heard of for old Boxer to shove someone like that off on me, and it's just another score I've got to settle with the son of a bitch if I ever get the chance.

All this time I kept on practicing basketball under Dilky in the old gym, and old Micky and I got to be just what he'd said we'd be, a real one-two punch, and as a matter of fact we got so sharp and good that Dilky got together with Barker Umplett and decided to change the kind of offense they'd been planning for the team. The way they'd planned it, they'd planned to use old Carboy under the bucket as the big scoring gun, but he was such a lousy shot, like I told, that they decided to use him there to get the ball and feed out to Micky and me for jump shots instead, and as a matter of fact it was something like Tizzy Davis and I had done it under old buller Mulloy, only a damn sight better. In December we started playing freshman teams from other schools, and we cleaned up everything around and looked plenty sharp, and it was a damn good thing old Umplett had something coming, if you want to know it, because as a matter of fact the varsity team wasn't so hot, and it was the first time in years old Umplett had had a lousy team. First of December, they made a tour through the East and played five games and lost three of them, and old Umplett could feel his throat bleeding and was sour and mean and hard to get along with.

Well, in spite of old Sylvia and a few other things I won't mention, the first year at Pipskill was pretty dull, as you can see, and after the freshman team got through beating all the other freshman teams around, there wasn't a hell of a lot of use hanging on, except that the living was pretty good, a hell of a lot better than anywhere else as a matter of fact, and besides, I had to finish out the term if I wanted to come back and play basketball in the fall, so I did.

The varsity team wasn't so hot, like I said, but old Umplett really worked the hell out of them when they got back from the eastern swing, and it looked for a while like he was going to bring them out of it, and the truth is, he damn near did, and after Christmas, when conference play started, they went into a winning streak and went right on winning all their games up to the last three, and damned if they didn't drop all of those in a row. That knocked them right out of the conference championship and the right to play in the national tournaments that came afterward, and old Umplett just blew his God-damn stack, because a coach at Pipskill that didn't win the conference and get in the national tournaments afterward was damn well liable not to be around long. It made it tough on us guys on the freshman team, because next season we'd be on the varsity, and old Umplett had blood in his eye and would be expecting us to save his God-damn hide for him, and just before we knocked off practice in the old gym, Dilky got us all together and told us that was the way it was and that we damn well better produce if we knew what was good for us.

That was in March, and I hung on a couple of months or so, a little longer, until school quit in June, and then I went home for the summer. The old man was at work when I got there, and the old lady said, "Well, I see you've come back to sponge off your old man some more. What's the matter? They quit feeding you up there at the college?" and I said, "That's a hell of a God-damn welcome to get when you've been gone damn near a whole year," and she said, "Welcome! Look who the hell's yakking about welcome. You never wrote to us or sent us a dime all that time you were up there and the minute your belly gets empty you come running home yelling welcome. You expect me to fall on your neck or something?" and I said, "The only place I expect you to fall is on your God-damn face from always swilling that lousy beer," and she said, "You wouldn't talk to me like that if only Eddy was here," and right away we were off on that crummy routine, and she started to bawl, and I wished to hell I hadn't come home at all, and to tell the truth, I wouldn't have if the hundred clams a month had kept on during the summer, but they didn't.

When the old man got home from work, he looked at me and said, "Where the hell you been?" and I said, "Been? You know God-damn well where I've been. I've been up to Pipskill going to school and playing basketball, that's where I've been," and he said, "Don't hand me that. The God-damn school closes up for Christmas, at least. Why the hell didn't you come home for Christmas? You afraid you'd have to buy someone a present or something?" and I said, "Now isn't that a crying shame! Since when did anyone in this crummy family ever buy anyone else a Christmas present? What the hell's the matter with you, anyway? You know damn well you don't give a damn if I come home for Christmas or any other time, and the way it looks to me, it looks like you'd rather I wouldn't, as a matter of fact."

He looked at me for a minute without saying anything, and then he said, "Well, now, maybe that's just the God-damn way it is, now that you mention it, and I'll tell you something else, too. Your old lady and I know you been getting paid a hundred dollars a month to play basketball up there at Pipskill, so there's no use trying to tell us any of your God-damn lies about it, and if you're planning to louse around here all summer, you'll damn well pay board, and that's all of it."

"You're crazy as hell," I said. "They don't pay me anything during the summer," and he said, "They sure as hell paid you something during the winter, and you better have some of it left if you expect me to fill your belly any longer," and then the old lady jumped in and asked the old man who the hell he thought he was to be throwing her only son out of the God-damn house without asking her anything about it, and he was surprised at that, and so was I, to tell the truth, and he said, "Who the hell pulled *your* string?" and she said, "He cusses me and abuses me and breaks my heart and is a bum in general, but he's my own flesh and blood and poor Eddy's own brother, and I won't have him thrown out of the house," and he said, "Well, mother, maybe you'd like to pay for the God-damn chow he's going to eat," and they kept at it back and forth and forgot about me, and I went out in the kitchen and ate and got the hell out of there for a while, and the old man kept threatening to throw me out off and on all summer but never did.

I had an idea I'd pick up again with Marsha Davis, which would have made the summer something to tell about, but the high school had quit two weeks earlier than Pipskill, and by the time I got home she'd already gone off somewhere with her old lady, to some God-damn lake or somewhere, and she never got back while I was there, and as a matter of fact I

never did pick it up again, and I guess it was just as well in the long run, but I didn't think so at the time. For a while I loused around with old Bugs, as much as I could stand him, and the truth is, he was always making snotty remarks about big shots and stuff and how some guys got swelled heads over nothing, and it was a lot of crap in general because I made a special effort not to break it off in him, feeling kind of sorry for him because he was too damn dumb to go to college, but finally I got sick of it and knocked him on his tail, and that was the end of it. After that I shot a little rotation and stuff and went out to the high school and got permission to sharpen up my eye in the gym while no one else was using it, and nothing much happened until just a few days before it was time to go back to Pipskill, and it was then I got even with Gravy Dummke, and I'll have to tell about it.

It was one morning about nine o'clock, and I was walking along the street and just happened to look down this alley that went in back of Gravy's cigar store, and there was old Gravy up on a ladder looking over the edge of the building at the roof. I guess he'd been up there doing some work or something, and maybe had just stopped at the top of the ladder on his way down to see how it looked from there, but anyway he was just standing there, and I went down the alley fast and quiet and got between the ladder and the building and pushed the God-damn ladder over backwards. Old Gravy screamed like a crazy woman, honest to God, and you could have heard him a mile away, and he came down like a barrel of lard on the bricks, which is what the alley was made of, and I was a little scared at first because he didn't move, and I thought I'd killed him sure as hell, but it turned out he only had a concussion and broke his God-damn arm and was only in the hospital a couple of weeks.

Considering Gravy and everything, it was a good thing it was time to leave town, and I left and went back up to Pipskill and got set in the frat house with Micky, and we went around and reported to Barker Umplett in the field house when the time came. Most of last year's team had graduated, which was good riddance of bad rubbish, but there were a couple of guys left over who were seniors and pretty good, and it was plain enough right from the start that the first five would be

79

them and Micky and old Carboy and me. Old Carboy had practiced all summer on his hook shot, but it hadn't done him a hell of a lot of good, and usually when he tried to hook one over it was just the same as throwing the God-damn ball away, and old Umplett would stand him up like a kid in grade school, all seven feet of him, and he'd look at him for a while with his little eyes like a couple of nasty smears in his face, and then he'd start in a low voice to chew old Carboy out, and when it came to chewing old buller Mulloy and even Dilky had been sissies compared to Umplett. He always talked low and never bellowed or threw himself around like Mulloy had done, but he never had any prejudice against cussing, and more than anything he actually said, it was the tone of his voice that counted. He *sounded* like he hated your guts, and his little eyes *looked* like he hated your guts, and as a matter of fact he sure as hell *did*. I found out about that a couple of weeks after we'd started practicing, and this is the way I found it out.

I was on my way to practice, and I stopped in this place called the Pink Pig, which was a place just off the campus where a lot of us guys hung out and bought malts and stuff, and I happened to run into this girl I knew, name of Ellen, and I set up a malt for her, and she said, "I just happen to have the old man's car at school this week, Skimmer. How about running out to the Barn for a couple of beers?" Well, the Barn was a place out on the highway about a mile, and I said, "I haven't got time. I got to get to basketball practice," and she said, "Basketball practice? You rather go to basketball practice than out to the Barn with me? I must be slipping," and I said, "It's not that. It's just that old Umplett gets pretty mean when you miss practice," and she laughed and said, "Oh, if you're afraid of getting your wrist slapped, you can just forget I asked you."

"Who the hell's afraid?" I said, and she said, "It looks to me like you are," and I said, "Well, I'm ready to go out to the Barn any time you are, and I'll tell you right now you better have more than a couple of beers to offer, too," and she laughed and said, "That's the way I like to hear you talk. Rough and ready," and that was no lie, because she did like it and was pretty much that way herself, and whenever you were with old Ellen you could count on going on from a couple of beers to other things, and she always knew what she wanted and didn't mind letting you know it, a lot like Marsha had been and nothing at all like old Sylvia, who had been a cry baby besides being crazy.

Anyhow, I went on out to the Barn with Ellen and missed practice, and when I got back to the frat house that night, old Micky was flopped on the bed looking at some cheesecake in a magazine, and he said, "Where the hell you been?" and I said, "Out with Ellen, and if you want to put your asbestos ear muffs on, I'll tell you about it," and he said, "Asbestos ear muffs, hell! You better have an asbestos tail at practice tomorrow, because old Umpy's going to chew it good."

"Well," I said, "if he messes with me, he'll think he's got a God-damn wildcat by the tail," but I didn't put much heart in it because, as a matter of fact, I didn't feel much, and when I went around to practice the next afternoon I'll have to admit I was as nervous as a pregnant spinster. Old Umplett didn't look at me or say anything or do any God-damn thing at all, and that made it even worse, and all the time practice was going on I kept wondering when the hell he'd start in on me, and what with thinking about it all the time, I fumbled some passes and missed some easy shots and was pretty lousy altogether. He still didn't say anything, though, even when I loused up the plays, and afterward in the locker room I got to feeling easier and began to think maybe I was going to get away with it all right, and of course that's just when the son of a bitch reached out and grabbed me.

I'd just finished dressing, and he stuck his bald head out the door of his stinking little office and said, "Come in here, Scaggs," and there wasn't a damn thing I could do but go. I went in and stood there with my teeth hanging out, and he sat down in the chair behind his desk and slumped down on the back of his neck and looked at me through his God-damn eyebrows and didn't ask me to sit down or drop dead or anything at all. He just sat there looking at me like it made him sick to his stomach to do it, and after a while I got to feeling all squirmy inside like I was full of worms, and I said, "You want to talk to me, Coach?" and he said, "No. The last thing on God's earth I want to do is talk to you, so I'm going to make it short and to the point."

I could see then that he was feeling pretty mean, which

81

wasn't anything unusual, and pretty soon he said, "Where the hell were you yesterday?" and I said, "I had something else I had to do," and he got a little smile on his face and kept looking at me with his nasty eyes that looked half asleep, and after about a full God-damn minute, he said, "Now isn't that interesting! Isn't that just about the most interesting God-damn thing you could imagine! Well, Mr. Scaggs, I'm sure an important fellow like you just has a lot of things to do that might interfere with basketball practice, so I think I'd better tell you how I feel about it. To put it bluntly, Mr. Scaggs, if your God-damn grandmother dropped dead at your feet at five minutes to three, I'd expect you to be to practice at three sharp as usual. Is that clear? While I'm at it, I might say that I've been in this business more years than I can count, and I've had my head on the chopping block more times than I care to remember, and I've learned a hell of a lot of things a man has to know to stay hooked to a contract, and one of the things I've learned is the smell of a sharp little opportunist like you. By God, you're just barely dry behind the ears, and you're already making a business out of what was once meant to be fun. So it's a business. It's business with you, and it's business with me, and there's no God-damn fun left in it. You're getting paid to come to school to play basketball, and you wouldn't ever come to school at all if you *didn't* get paid to play basketball, and so you'll God-damn well *play* basketball. You'll come to practice after this on time and every time, and you'll run and you'll sweat and you'll hate my guts, and the more you hate them the better I'll like it, and don't ever expect me to treat you like anything but the hired sharpshooter you are. You're paid to win games, and that's exactly what I expect of you and nothing more, and God help you if you don't. Is all this perfectly clear, Mr. Scaggs?"

Well, it sure as hell was, and I said so and left, and after that it would have taken a hell of a lot more than a few beers and what I could find in a pair of drawers to make me miss a practice, and to tell the truth, I didn't miss another damn one, and whatever else he was, old Umplett was the best damn basketball coach that ever lived, and I'll admit it even though I hated his guts just like he said I would.

He worked the hell out of us all through November, and we

82

got faster and faster, and the faster we got the smoother we got, and even old Carboy quit falling over his own feet all the time and got pretty good at jumping up and ramming one through from the rafters now and then, but mostly he took the ball in the slot and fed out to Micky or me, and there weren't any flies on that Micky, either, if you want to know the truth of it, and you could tell that God-damn Umplett was looking forward to a good season but would rather have dropped dead than say so.

Toward the end of November we had a couple of home games scheduled, and these were just with small colleges not far away and not very good, and we won them both by scores that looked like the totals in some lopsided election or something. You wouldn't have thought a couple of crummy games like that would get much play, but anyone who thought like that just didn't know Pipskill, and they'd have turned out for a game there if it had been with some team scraped up in a kindergarten. The field house was packed, and the band played, and all in all it was just like the old high school, except bigger and louder and even crazier. As a matter of fact, I never saw such blood-thirsty God-damn maniacs in my life, and even when we had the score almost doubled they kept yelling at us to pour it on and kept cheering every lousy point like it might make the difference between winning and losing. Lots of coaches will ease up a little when their team gets a big lead, but not old Umplett. He kept the first stringers in right up to the end, and maybe it was because the crowd wanted him to and he knew damn well better, but it was more likely because he was just as blood-thirsty as any bastard in the crowd, and however it was, it was great stuff for your point total, and I made forty points the first game and thirty-five the second, and right after that everyone started calling me the Platinum Sophomore, which is what they kept on calling me all year, even in the newspapers.

First part of December, we made a swing through the East all the way to New York and played two games on the way and one in Madison Square Garden and one on the way back, and we won all the games but not by any God-damn lopsided scores like the first two at home. As a matter of fact we damn near lost the one in Madison Square Garden because we had

83

a fat lead at the half and got sloppy in the third quarter while the other team was getting hot, and we were lucky to pull it out by three points at the end. Old Umplett was so God-damn mad about it that he jerked us all back to the hotel and wouldn't let us go out and see some of the town, and Micky and I talked about sneaking out to see some of it, anyhow, but decided not to.

The next morning we started home and stopped off for the last game, and this game was with a college that hadn't lost a game on their home court for about a million years, and I guess no one around there thought they were *ever* going to lose one, but we changed a hell of a lot of thinking on that subject before we were through with them. The God-damn people who came to watch the game were just as crazy as the people at Pipskill, and when the game was almost over and they began to realize how it was coming out, they started to boo us and throw paper and stuff on the court and raise hell in general, and damned if it didn't look for a while like they might lynch us or something, but we got out of it all right and left town the next day. I read later on in the sports page that they said the only reason we beat them was because their star player had a stinking virus or something and was sick and played the whole game on the verge of death like a God-damn hero, and we couldn't beat them again in a thousand years, but this was just sour grapes and a damn lie, and we proved it by beating them again in a tournament after the regular season was over, and I made ten more points than their lousy hero to boot.

When we got back to the university station on the train, the band was there and about a thousand people, and they made a hell of a fuss about damn little, it seemed to me, but I was glad they did because it reminded me that this basketball racket was a pretty big thing and worth taking care of, and old Umplett made a speech on the platform about how last year had been a long dry spell as far as basketball was concerned, but this year looked like being a hell of a lot greener.

Well, he was right about that, and it sure as hell was, and after the Christmas holiday, which I spent at the frat house again, we got started on conference play and won two fast games. There's not a hell of a lot of use telling all about the games we played, as far as I can see, because basketball may be fun to watch, especially if you got a band playing and some good-looking dolls leading cheers and stuff and giving you a chance to raise some general hell, but I can't help thinking it would be pretty damn dull reading about, and to tell the truth I wouldn't spend a minute myself reading about a lot of guys running up and down a court trying to throw a ball through a hoop. Anyhow, I'll just tell you that we went through the damn conference like a dose of salts and never lost a game, and when the season was about half over we were rated number one team in the entire country by those so-called experts who go in for that kind of stuff, the sports writers and spooks like that, but to tell the truth I wasn't much impressed by it because it seemed to me they just sat around and waited to see who won most of the games and then made a big production out of saying these were the best teams, and as far as I can see almost anyone could be a God-damn expert at something like that.

Winning the conference meant we got to play in the regional tournament after the regular season and got to go on and play in the national finals if we won the regional, and the closer we got to the time to play the meaner old Umplett got in the way he acted and talked, and he said he didn't see how the hell we'd ever get past the first game, and the only reason we were in the tournament in the first place was because the conference had been so God-damn weak, and it just made him sick to his crummy stomach to think what jackasses we were going to look when those sharp teams from the other conferences turned loose on us, but none of us believed a damn word he said, and he didn't, either. We had almost two weeks between the last conference game and the tournament, and the last week of practice was pretty light because old Umplett was afraid we might go stale if we overdid it, and it was during this time I met this guy named Arnold Hamshank, and since I got a good job for the summer and a little red Crosley out of him, I better tell you why it was.

The simple truth is, he was a God-damn fool about basketball, and as a matter of fact he was probably the biggest fool about basketball I ever met, and I guess I've met them about as big as they come. The way I met him, I went into the city with old Carboy and Micky one evening to see a doll named

Zalita at a burlesque show who was supposed to be hot stuff, but the truth is, she must have been someone's grandmother at least, and she reminded me of the doll in the joke who tried to shoot herself under the left breast and blew off her kneecap. After the show we went to a place to buy a steak and sneak a beer, and this Hamshank was there and came over to our table.

"Aren't you Carboy, Spicer and Scaggs?" he said, and we said we were, and he said, "Congratulations on winning the conference championship," and we said thanks, and he said, "Now for the national championship, and I know you can do it because you've got the best damn team in the whole country, which is the same as saying in the whole world."

The way it turned out, he sat down at our table and began talking all about basketball and stuff, and he knew all the good players from back when they first started playing the God-damn game, including all the statistics for practically anyone you cared to mention, including me, and as a matter of fact he was a real God-damn maniac about the crazy game, and a funny thing was, he didn't particularly look like he would be. I mean he was a big fat guy with a lot of gray hair and a kind of dignified look about him, except for being a little red in the face, and you might have thought he was a lousy judge or someone who didn't go in for light stuff like basketball, but the truth was, he had an automobile agency and sold Packards and Crosleys. After we'd talked a while, he picked up the check and said he'd pay it, and we told him he didn't have to do it but didn't argue a hell of a lot about it, and he said he really wanted to do it as a kind of gesture to three of the greatest little old players in the country, and what was more, he was ready to give a brand new red Crosley sports car to the man on the team who wound up high point man in the tournament. I thought at first the old son of a bitch was drunk, but I couldn't smell anything on him, and I decided that he was really serious, the goofy bastard, and that I'd sure as hell have that red Crosley or my name wasn't Skimmer Scaggs, which it sure as hell was.

Well, I might as well tell you right off that we didn't win the national tournament that year. Maybe you remembered it and how it was, but if you don't, it was this way. We won the regional, all right, and went right on through the national

86

finals to the last game, and damned if we didn't get beat by a lousy team that no one had thought would even get out of the regionals, let alone win the finals, and the reason was, they were just as hot as God-damn firecrackers, and that's one of the goofy things about basketball, especially in tournaments. What I mean, a team that ordinarily wouldn't show a chance will catch fire and play over their heads for a few games, and in a tournament a few games are plenty, and that's the way it was with this team. It seemed like they couldn't miss the God-damn bucket for any reason whatever, and every time someone grabbed the damn ball and fired away from practically any place on the court, it just dropped through with a little swish of the net, and altogether it was enough to break your damn heart. They beat us by six points and were national champions, but I was high point man of the game and of the whole damn tournament, as a matter of fact, so I didn't feel as bad as I might have otherwise, and I planned to go around to Arnold Hamshank's place just as soon as I got back to find out if he really meant it about the red Crosley or was just a damn liar.

The truth is, he was a hell of a windbag, especially when he got onto basketball and started telling you how you should have done something this way or that way or any God-damn way but the way you did it, but he wasn't a liar and had meant what he said and came across with the Crosley like it was nothing but a scooter. I went down to his display room a couple of days after I got back, and it was a real fancy place right downtown on a corner with three slick Packards and a lot of green plants and things behind about a million square feet of plate glass. When I went in a guy came up to me rubbing his hands together, and he asked me what I wanted, and I said I wanted to see Mr. Hamshank, and he said he was sorry but Mr. Hamshank wasn't in right then but would be back soon. I said I'd wait and went around and looked at the three Packards and thought to myself that maybe I'd have one myself one of these days if this basketball racket kept on growing the way it had been so far, but for the time being I was just concentrating on that God-damn red Crosley. It was maybe half an hour later when Mr. Hamshank got there, and he saw me looking at the Packards and recognized me right away and came over and said, "Well, well, Skimmer, welcome, my boy.

Tough luck about the tournament, but better luck next year."
I said hello and that I was glad he remembered me, and he
said how the hell could he forget the best forward in the country who was on practically everyone's All-American team even
as a sophomore, which I was, and he asked me to come into
his office and sit down, and we went in and did.

"How the hell did it happen?" he said, and I said, "What?"
and he said, "Why, that last game. How the hell did that scrub
team ever happen to beat you?"

"It was just one of those things," I said. "They just got hot
and couldn't miss the basket any way they tried, and you know
how it is with a team like that, there just isn't anything you can
do to stop them, because if they bent over and fired the damn
ball between their legs it would still go in," and he said, "That's
the damn truth, but just the same, if I'd been coach instead of
Umplett . . . ," and then he went on telling me what he'd have
done if he'd been coach, and it was a lot of crap, of course,
and it took him damn near a half hour to get through with it,
and I'd just about decided that he was just giving me a God-
damn runaround and was trying to talk about anything but the
red Crosley he owed me, but then he wound up saying, "But
however it might have been, it's water under the bridge now,
and the fact is, you were high point man of the tournament
and have won the Crosley sports car."

"Well," I said, "I don't expect you to give me anything as
valuable as a Crosley sports car. Besides, I never thought for
a minute you really meant it," and he said, "The hell I didn't
mean it. When Arnold Hamshank says he'll do a thing, he'll
damn sure do it, and the car's greased and oiled and full of
gas and ready to go in the back room right now."

I said that was sure as hell generous of him, and it was sure
swell to know someone who liked basketball well enough to do
something like that to encourage one of the players, and he said
to think nothing of it and that he was always ready to do a little
thing now and then for the boys who made the game what it
was, and to tell the truth, I thought he was a damn fool to put
out a new Crosley to someone like me that he didn't even really
know just for throwing a God-damn ball around. Anyhow, he
asked me if I'd like to go back and take a look at it, and I said
I would, and we went back and looked it over, and it was sure

88

as hell little, just a one-seater like all sports cars, bright red and shiny as a new nickel, and I thought it was a damn sweet little job but that you'd sure never get any business done in the seat like old Marsha Davis and I had almost got done in the front seat of her old man's Buick.

He said, "Well, what do you think of it?" and I said it was a slick little job, and we went back to his office again, and he had all the papers and everything already fixed up for me to sign and all I had to do was get a driver's license and buy some tags and I was all set. We talked some more about other things, and after a while he said, "Where's your home, Skimmer?" and I told him, and he said, "That's not a very big town, is it?" and I said it sure as hell wasn't, and he said, "It must be pretty dull for a guy like you around there in the summer," and I said it sure as hell was.

"How'd you like to stay here in the city this summer?" he said, and I said I'd like it fine but didn't have the money, and he said, "You could get a job, couldn't you?" and I had to admit I hadn't thought of that, and he said, "How'd you like to work for me selling cars?"

"Well," I said, "I'd like that fine, but I never sold cars before," and he said, "There's nothing to it. A big basketball star like you would be a cinch, because people around here go in a big way for basketball players. I'd pay you fifty bucks a week plus commission," and I said, "That sounds good to me, and you've just hired yourself a salesman for the summer," and he said, "That's the stuff. I like a guy who can make up his mind in a hurry, and I knew you could do it because you wouldn't be the best forward in the country if you couldn't. That's one thing about basketball, it teaches you to make up your mind fast."

After a while I said I had to be getting back to the university, and he said to drop in and see him once in a while, and I said I would, and he said he'd be expecting me to start work right after school was out in June, and I said I'd do that, too. He followed me back to the Crosley and watched me crawl in and start it up, and he laughed and waved and yelled as I drove out to be sure to remember to get out of the Crosley before I got into the mood, and I yelled back that I would and drove on out, and I was feeling damn good, I don't mind admitting, not only

89

because I had the Crosley but because I had a job for the summer, too, and wouldn't have to go home and put up with the bull from the old man just to get a crummy meal now and then.

That was how it happened that I stayed in the city that summer, and if it hadn't been for old Arnold Hamshank giving me the job selling cars I'd probably have gone on home and never met Candy Caldwell or Francis Z. Ketch, who was called Franzie because of everyone's running his first name and middle initial together like one word, or any of the others that I met. Everything goes right back to that God-damn crazy game of basketball, and it just seems impossible that so much could have come of it, but that's the way it was, and it's a good thing for me I learned to play it. Candy Caldwell was the one I met first, and I didn't meet this Franzie Ketch for quite a while afterward, because he wasn't the kind of guy you met easy, and as a matter of fact you didn't meet him at all unless you had something he wanted, which I did, and so I'll start with Candy and work through it the way it came.

After school was out I went down and took over the job selling cars, and it was a pretty damn plush job, if you ask me, because old Hamshank didn't seem to give a damn whether I put in much time selling or not, and every now and then he'd come around and say, "Skimmer there's a guy I know ought to be about ready for a new Packard. This guy's a hot basketball fan, so why don't you run out and see him," and so I'd run out and see this guy he told me about, and usually he'd get warmed up right away when he found out who I was and wind up a little later taking the Packard, which meant a commission on top of the fifty bucks, and altogether it was just like sitting under a tree in the shade and having someone shake apples in your lap. I got me a room in a little hotel that didn't cost too much but wasn't a bad place to flop, and this hotel was right at the edge of the downtown area where a lot of nightclubs and things were, and I got to going down there nights to see the shows and learned how to drink stuff like martinis and daiquiris and not always plain beer, and you'd be surprised how many people I met who knew me from all the publicity I'd got over the basketball and wanted to give me the glad hand and buy me a drink and things like that.

One afternoon a little after five o'clock I went into a cocktail lounge called the Gay Gander that was a pretty fancy place with a thick carpet and big pots of green stuff here and there and soft light coming out of a little trough that went all around the room up near the ceiling. I was sitting by myself at a table, because all the stools at the bar had roosters on them, and all of a sudden this guy with slick black hair stepped out with a little microphone and said, "Ladies and gentlemen, here she is," just like any damn fool ought to know who *she* was, and I guess most of them did, even if I didn't, because they started to clap in the quiet way they do it in joints like that, and another guy came out and sat down at a piano, and this doll followed him and leaned against the piano and began to sing. She was wearing a black dress that was made out of thin stuff that showed the black slip underneath, and it came down to just below her knees at the bottom and down to damn near below her knockers on top, and her hair was black, too, and cut short and sort of shaggy on purpose, and I'd like to describe the rest of her, just the way she looked, but I damn sure can't, and no one else could, either.

Well, it was this Candy Caldwell I mentioned, and she sang these little songs that weren't dirty in exactly what they said but were damn sure dirty in what they meant, especially the way she sang them, and everyone in the place just ate it up, including me. As a matter of fact, I never had a doll get to me the way she did, not even old Marsha, and I sat there and watched her for all the half hour she was on and wished it was longer. When she'd finished and gone, a waitress came up to my table and asked me if I wanted another drink, which I did, and I asked her the name of the doll who sang the songs, and she said, "Why, that's Candy Caldwell," and she said it with this snotty look like she thought anyone would have to be pretty damn ignorant not to know who Candy Caldwell was, and I said, "Well, I'd sure like to have her sing some of those songs to me personally," and she said, "You and a million others, sonny. Give it up. She's got connections, and she comes high," and that just showed how damn ignorant this snotty waitress was herself, because she didn't even know that I was a big basketball star with connections of my own, which was just as bad in its way as not knowing who Candy Caldwell was. Anyhow, I asked her if Candy Caldwell was going to sing any more songs later, and she said yes, a hell of a lot later, about nine o'clock that night as a matter of fact, and I made up my mind right then and there that I'd be back at nine o'clock to see her do it, and I was.

The second time was even better than the first time, and she was dressed in a white dress that came all the way to the floor at the bottom, instead of just below her knees, but came down to about the same place as the black one at the top, which was about as far down as it could go without being nothing but a skirt. She sang for a half hour again, all these little songs that meant more than they really said, and when she quit I decided I might as well take the God-damn bull by the horns and called a waitress over and told her to go tell Candy Caldwell that Skimmer Scaggs would like to meet her, and it cost me a lousy fin to get the waitress to go. I sat there and waited for a while, and pretty soon someone came up to my table, but it wasn't Candy Caldwell. It was a tall guy with blond hair brushed straight back over his head with the scalp showing through, it was so God-damn thin, and he had a kind of narrow, mean face with a little smile on it that didn't help much. I thought at first maybe he was going to throw me out on my ass for trying to get to meet Candy Caldwell, but it turned out he was friendly and said, "Are you Skimmer Scaggs, the basketball star?"

I said I was, and he said, "Sure glad to meet you, Scaggs. I'm Hershell Goans. I manage this place," and I said I was glad to meet him, too, which was just a way of speaking and not particularly true because the only person I really wanted to meet was Candy Caldwell, and he must have read my mind because he said, "I understand you'd like to meet our little singer."

I said I sure as hell would, and he laughed and said, "Well, a lot of guys would like to do that, and she usually doesn't give any house to strangers, but I'm pretty sure she'd be willing to make an exception of a famous athlete like you. I'll tell you what. You just sit here and take it easy, and I'll go back and see if she won't come out and have a drink with you."

He went away to get her, and I sat there waiting, and they didn't come for so long that I'd just about decided they were only making a God-damn monkey out of me, but then they came, and this guy Goans said, "Skimmer, meet Candy Caldwell. You're in luck, boy. It just happens Candy's quite a fan of yours," and I stood up and said, "No bull?" and she laughed and said, "That's right, Skimmer. I was just too excited when Hersh told me you were out here and wanted to meet me."

She sat down, and I did, too, and Hershell Goans called a waitress over and said anything we wanted was on the house, and I couldn't help wishing it was the snotty bitch who'd waited on me in the afternoon, but it wasn't. Candy ordered a martini, and I said I'd have the same, and Goans said, "You kids have fun," and went away, which was the best thing he could have done as far as I was concerned. I tried to think of something fancy to say, but damned if I could think of a thing, and to tell the truth, I was too busy looking things over right at first, anyhow, and it seemed to be all right with her. She was still wearing the white dress she'd worn to sing in, and she sat there smiling a little and fiddling with the stem of her martini glass, and pretty soon she said, "Well, you like it?" and I said, "What?" and she said, "What you're looking at," and I said, "What you mean, it? There are *two* of them," and as a matter of fact, it just slipped out, and I was afraid at first that I'd fouled the nest, but she thought it was funny and said, "My God, you're *really* a fast worker, aren't you?"

After that I felt as loose as ashes, and I started talking about basketball and asking her questions, because this Hershell Goans who managed the place had said she was a fan and I thought she'd be interested, but the truth is, she didn't seem to know a damn thing about basketball, and I decided that maybe she wasn't exactly a fan of the game but was just a fan of mine personally. The way it turned out, though, she wasn't really any kind of fan at all, and after a while she laughed and said, "Look, honey, don't get sore about it, but I don't know a damn thing about basketball and care less and I've never seen a game in my life. The way it was, I looked out and saw you sitting here, and I thought you were cute, and all that stuff about being a fan was just an angle. You know how it is."

I said sure, I knew how it was, and as a matter of fact I wouldn't have been a fan of the God-damn crazy game myself if I hadn't got to playing it by accident. She asked me how I got started, and I told her about the time old Bugs bet me his lousy two-bits that I couldn't hit two out of ten, and how I went on after that and became the best player in the state and got an athletic scholarship to Pipskill, and how I was thinking about going ahead and getting on a pro team after college, because I'd heard that was a good racket, too. She said I must really be good, and I said I sure as hell was, and she said she liked men who were good at things, no matter what they were, and I said she might be surprised how good I was at certain things *besides* basketball, and she laughed and patted my hand and said, "Jesus Christ, what a *busy* little man you are. Always in there trying."

We had a couple more drinks after the first one, and I asked her if she'd like to go somewhere in my Crosley, and she said, "In your what?" and I said, "In my Crosley, God-damn it," and she said, "You mean one of these little tiny cars?" and I said, "Well, it's pretty small, all right, but it's a red one-seater, a kind of sports car, and all sports cars are supposed to be small," and she said, "Oh, a sports car! I love sports cars. I'll tell you what. I've got to go on for another half hour spot at eleven, but if you'll hang around until after that, I'll let you take me home."

I said I'd hang around, all right, and I did, and we kept on sitting there and talking and having a fresh martini every once in a while, and about a quarter to eleven she got up and said, "I've got to get ready for my next spot now, honey. Don't go away," and that was a God-damn laugh because you couldn't have drug me away from there with a team of mules, and I'll admit that the gin was working on me pretty good and I had about three sheets in the wind. Candy came on and sang her songs, and she picked out the most suggestive one of all to sing right to me, and everyone could tell what she was doing, and a few people started to laugh and clap a little, and I sure didn't give a damn. The song was one where some doll was in a hot spot with some guy, and she kept saying don't and stop, and pretty soon she got to saying them so close together that it sounded like she was saying don't stop, and I thought, Well, you can just bet your pretty tail I won't.

When she'd finished singing, she disappeared for a while, and I had another martini on the house while I was waiting for

94

her to show up, and when she came she was in a street dress instead of the long white one she'd been wearing, but I was so fogged up with gin by that time that I don't remember just what it looked like except that it was enough to knock your eye out, just like all the other dresses she wore.

"You ready to go, honey?" she said, and I said I was and stood up and damn near fell on my face, and she laughed and said, "Who the hell's taking who home?"

She took my arm, and we went out, and when we passed this guy Hershell Goans, he laughed and said, "Take good care of our basketball hero, baby," and Candy said, "Oh, I'll take care of him, all right," and then we got outside on the sidewalk and walked down to where I'd parked the Crosley, and she said, "Well, isn't it cute! Does it have an engine, or do you pump it with your feet?" and I said, "You just crawl in the God-damn seat, and I'll show you if it's got an engine or not," and she said, "Nix, honey, I'm too young to die. You just crawl in like a good boy, and I'll drive this gadget myself."

I argued about it a little, but she said I'd damn well let her drive or we'd just call the whole thing off, and so finally I got in the seat and she went around and got under the wheel and drove us to the apartment house where she lived. It was a medium fancy place with one of these awning things running from the front entrance to the curb for you to walk under, and Candy pulled into a parking space at the curb just below the awning and cut the engine and said, "Look, honey, you're in pretty bad shape. I've got an electric pot and some coffee up-stairs. You want to come up with me, I'll fix you up," and I said, "Is that a promise?" and she laughed and patted my cheek and said, "My God, you're about the *busiest* sophomore I ever ran into," and I said I wasn't any God-damn sophomore, but a junior, and she said, "Okay, Junior, come along," which I did and had intended to do, anyhow, coffee or no coffee.

We went up in the elevator and down to her apartment and inside, and it was a nice place with some modern-looking furniture standing around on black wrought-iron legs. She was holding me by the arm when we went in, and as soon as the door closed behind us she swung around in front of me and put her arms up around my neck, and I put mine around her down where it counted for more, and we started kissing, and

95

that went on for a while, and then she stepped back and laughed this shaky laugh and said, "Well, well, Junior, you're not only cute, but talented. Maybe this caper will turn out to be more fun than business."

I started to grab her again, but she put her hand against my chest and held me off and said, "Let's build it up as we go along, Junior. It's better that way," and I thought I might as well play it by her rules and let her go, and she walked over toward a door that led into a bedroom and said over her shoulder, "Sit down and take it easy, honey. I'll be back in a minute," and it wasn't much longer than that before she was, and I sat on a sofa and waited and thought about all the stories I'd read, especially about private eyes, how the doll walks off to the bedroom saying something like that and comes back pretty soon naked or in a God-damn thin robe or something, and I wondered if that was the way it was going to be with Candy, and hoped it was, but it wasn't. She still had the same dress on and hadn't done a damn thing to herself as far as I could see, and she walked over to a chest and took out a couple of bottles and glasses and mixed drinks and carried them over to me and handed me one and said, "Since you probably won't be driving home tonight after all, we can just skip the coffee, can't we?"

Well, I guess I was pretty tight, but I was still able to tell when I'd had an invitation, and I took the glass and said we sure as hell could, and she sat down beside me real close and said, "Tell me all about yourself," and I couldn't see a hell of a lot of use wasting time on it and said so, but she took a swallow of her drink and said, "For God's sake, Junior, don't push it so hard. We got all night."

I took a big swallow of my drink and damn near choked to death, it was so damn strong, and my head got to going around and around all of a sudden, and I tried to think of some good lies to tell her about my family and who I was and everything, but I couldn't seem to get going on it, and then I had this feeling that there wouldn't be any percentage in telling lies about it to Candy, anyhow, because it wouldn't make any damn difference to her at all like it might have made to old Marsha, and so I just told her the truth about everything, about the old man and the old lady and how I'd pushed the ladder over

96

with Gravy Dummke on it, and she laughed and laughed and thought it was funny as hell. When I was finished I thought it might make me some points if I acted like I wanted to know everything about her, too, not that I cared a hell of a lot about it, and so I asked her to tell me all about her God-damn life and stuff, and she said, "Junior, I haven't had any life. I just started to live when I met you tonight."

This was bull, and I knew it, and she said, "Is your name really Skimmer?" and I said it sure as hell was and was her name really Candy, and she said, "Christ, no. Who the hell ever named a kid Candy?" and I asked her what her real name was, then, and she said it was Myrtle, if I wanted to know, but she'd changed it to Candy because who the hell would come to a cocktail lounge to hear a girl named Myrtle sing songs? I said as far as I was concerned I'd come to hear her sing if her name was Mud, and she said that was a sweet thing to say, and it got us started on a pretty good tussle that led from one thing to another, and pretty soon she stood up and said, "Let's go in the other room," meaning the bedroom, and I stood up to go and fell on my lousy face. She laughed and helped me up and into the bedroom and told me to sit down on the bed and she'd be right back. I sat down and heard her in the bathroom, and my head was going around this way, and I remember lying down on my back for just a second until she came, and damned if I didn't pass out and not come to until the next day, which was the damnedest thing I ever did.

When I came around I was still lying on the God-damn bed, but I didn't have anything on but my stinking shorts and was lying around the long way instead of crossways, and I had a hell of a headache, and my mouth tasted like I had my socks in it. No one was on the bed but me, but I could tell that some-one *had* been on it, and there was a racket going on somewhere that turned out to be the shower in the bathroom, and pretty soon Candy came out in a blue robe and said, "Well, Junior, how you feeling?" and I said I felt like hell, a little from the gin and whisky, but mostly because I'd missed the lousy bus, and she said I sure as hell had and started to laugh about it.

"Well," I said, "you miss the first bus, you can always catch one later," and she came over and sat down on the edge of the bed beside me and said, "Look, honey, you're a cute kid, and all this business about your being a star basketball player and everything is just too precious, but now it's the morning after the night that was almost before, and it's time to look at the facts. What I mean is, it looked like it might be fun, so I gave you a free pass for one ride, but I can't make a habit of it. To put it bluntly, Junior, I like to go lots of places and do lots of things and wear lots of what makes a girl pretty, including precious stones, and I've got to save my time and talent for the guys who can afford to give me what I like."

That was laying it on the line, all right, and it was fine with me, and I said, "Maybe I got more in the sock than you think," and she said, "If you got more than your foot in it, it'd damn sure be more than I think. Tell me, Junior. How much you making out of this damn game?"

"Well," I said, "I'm only getting a hundred a month to play out at Pipskill, but there are things on the side," and she said, "Such as?" and I said, "Such as fifty bucks a week plus commissions from Hamshank's Automobile Agency," and she laughed and patted my cheek in the way she had and said, "You see? You don't even know the meaning of big dough. In a way it's a shame, too, because you're cute and I really go for you and there ought to be ways a guy in your position could cash in."

The way I looked at it, I didn't want this to slip away from me without another chance at it, and I said, "Well, this basketball thing has room to grow. I've been thinking about quitting out at the university after this year and turning pro. Pros make a pot of dough if they're good enough," and she said, "Are you good enough?" and I said I sure as hell was, and she said, "Well, come around then and maybe we can pick it up again," and I said, "That's a year. Who the hell wants to wait a year?" and she smiled this little smile and reached up and let her fingers trail down my cheek, and all the time she was looking at me like she was trying to make up her mind whether she should say what she had on it or not, and after a long time she said, "Would you really like to make a potful, honey?"

As far as I could see, that was nothing but a foolish question, and I said I would, and she said, "Maybe I can put you in a way to do it," and I said, "How?" and she said, "There's a man

I know might be able to use you," and I said, "Who?" and she said, "His name is Francis Z. Ketch. You hear of him?" and I said I couldn't remember hearing of him but I'd be willing to see him if it meant getting in the way of making a potful, and she laughed and gave my cheek a last little pat and said it wasn't that easy, you didn't just go see Francis Z. Ketch, but that she'd work on it and try to arrange it.

The blue robe she was wearing didn't hide a hell of a lot, and I still had the idea of picking it up where we'd left it off, but she ducked away and clucked her tongue against her teeth in this cute way she had and stood up. This made me a little sore, if you want to know it, and I got up, too, and started to pull on my pants with the idea of getting the hell out of here, if that was the way she wanted it, and she stood there watching me and laughing a little, and after a second she said, "Don't get sore, honey. I'm strictly a night girl. In the daytime I just feel foolish."

Well, I felt pretty damn foolish myself, to tell the truth, standing there pulling on my pants and her laughing about it, and altogether it wasn't the kind of situation to make a guy look or feel his best by a damn sight. When I had all my clothes on, she came over and gave me another one of those pats on the cheek and said, "Do you really want me to see if I can get you an appointment with Franzie?" and I said, "Who the hell's Franzie?" and she said, "Why, Francis Z. Ketch, the man I told you about," and I said she could just suit herself as far as I was concerned, and she said I was still sore, and I said the hell I was, and she said, "Look, honey, don't be a damn baby about it. It just went sour on us this time, and it wouldn't be any good at all to try to pick it up now, but there's always the next time. How'd you like to come around to the Gay Gander and catch my songs tonight and bring me home afterward?"

Finally I said okay, I'd do it, and she said, "In the meantime I'll see if I can get Franzie to see you," and I said, "Why the hell do you call him Franzie?" and she told me this stuff about how his real close friends had called him Fran, and then someone had run it into the Z, and after that they called him Franzie as a result, and I said, "Are you one of his real close friends?" and she said, "Why? Jealous?" and I said why the hell

99

should I be jealous, and she said, "Maybe because you go for me," and I said I'd be a damn liar if I said I didn't, and next time, what was more, I was going all the way, and she said, "My *God,* how you *push!*"

After that I left and found a telephone and called Arnold Hamshank and told him I was sick as a dog and wouldn't be in to work, and he said it was okay, boy, to take good care of old Pipskill's most valuable player, and I went back to my room at the hotel and went to bed and didn't wake up until evening. I fooled around and did this and that until about ten o'clock and then went around to the Gay Gander, and Hershell Goans saw me at the bar where I was having a highball and came over and said, "Well, well, the big star's back again. You must like us here, boy," and I said I damn sure liked some of them at any rate, and he said, "You mean Candy?" and I said what did he think, and he laughed and thumped me on the shoulder and said, "Well, I don't mind telling you she seems to go for you, too, boy, and to tell the truth, it sort of surprises me because Candy's a high class dame with a million guys after her, more or less, and this is the first time I ever saw her go for one in a big way like this."

The bastard meant well and thought he was giving me a good word, but personally I couldn't see why the hell he should be so surprised about it, and to tell the truth, it made me kind of sore to hear him say it. I said thanks, though, I was glad he thought so, and I waited for him to tell the bartender to make everything on the house, like he'd done last night, but this time he didn't do it, and damned if I didn't have to pay for everything I drank, which was three highballs by the time Candy came on. She sang songs for half an hour, which was until eleven-thirty, and then it was another God-damn half hour before she came out to the bar, which made it twelve, and when we got outside to the Crosley, she said, "I tried to get Franzie to see you tonight, honey, but he said he couldn't do it and would try to find time for it some time later," and I said, "Well, isn't that just too God-damn big of him!"

She gave me this quiet look that was like she was trying to decide whether to tell you something or not, and pretty soon she said, "Look, Junior, you're a cute guy, and you've got more brass than an old-fashioned saloon, God knows, but take

100

my advice and don't go throwing your weight around with Franzie Ketch," and I said, "Well, I'm just scared to death," and she said, "You damn well better be," and I said, "I don't mind telling you I'm not afraid of anyone in the God-damn world, and I don't intend to wet my pants over this Ketch guy even if he's one of the big shots Gravy Dummke was supposed to know in the city," and she said, "Gravy Dummke? Who the hell's Gravy Dummke?" and I said he was the guy I'd told her about that was on the ladder I'd pushed over, and she said, "Well don't get any God-damn ideas about pushing any ladder over with Franzie Ketch on it."

To tell the truth, I was pretty sick of this God-damn Ketch character before I'd even met him, and didn't give much of a damn whether I *ever* met him or not, and I said, "Well, to hell with him. Just between the two of us, I didn't hit the booze at the Gay Gander so hard tonight, and I don't have any God-damn intention of passing out again, so I got better things to think about than some spook named Francis Z. Ketch, and you may not know it yet, but so have you."

She patted me and laughed and said, "Jesus, Junior, I wouldn't miss it for the world because there's just an outside chance you're maybe *half* as good as you think you are," and we drove on around to her apartment and went upstairs, and I had another drink but didn't pass out from it, and everything was different and a damn sight better than the night before. About three o'clock she told me I'd have to get the hell out, and I didn't want to go, but she said I'd damn well have to go whether I wanted to or not, and I could see she meant it, so I got ready and started, but at the door I turned and said, "I'll see you tonight at the Gay Gander," and she said, "The hell you will," and I said, "Why not?" and she said, "Listen, Junior, I got a soft spot in my heart where you're concerned, but don't get the idea I'm reorganizing my whole God-damn life to accommodate you. I'll work you into the schedule when I can, but that damn sure doesn't mean every night."

"Well," I said, "when's my next turn on the schedule?" and she said, "How the hell would I know? Didn't you ever hear of a telephone? Give me a ring sometime," and I could see that was the best I could get out of her right then, so I said I sure as hell would and went back to the hotel in the Crosley and went to bed. I didn't want to get up in the morning, but I thought I'd better get on around to Arnold Hamshank's just the same, so I went and when I came in he said, "Jesus, Skimmer, you really look pooped. You really must have been sick, boy," which was a damn belly-laugh, as you can see, but I didn't tell him why.

I thought I'd just let Candy sweat a little, since she was so damn independent, so I didn't call her for a couple of days, but when I finally called her on the third day I'm bound to admit she didn't seem to be in much of a sweat, and she told me she had other things to do and couldn't see me again until Saturday night, which was still two days away. I figured she was just playing hard to get, even though she'd already been got once, and to tell the truth, it made me a little hot, and I said well, it just happened I had something else to do Saturday night myself and couldn't make it, which was a damn lie, and she said, "Okay, Junior, have fun," and hung up.

I was in a sweat myself after that, and I finally decided there wasn't any use cutting off my nose to spite my God-damn face and called her again and said I'd found out I'd be able to make it to the Gay Gander after all and would be waiting for her after her eleven o'clock spot, and she said, "Well, it's lucky for you that you can make it, Junior, because I've finally got an appointment with Franzie Ketch for you, and he'll see you Saturday night. As a matter of fact, he wants me to bring you up to his place around ten, and I've got out of the eleven o'clock spot to do it, so you be at the Gander by nine-thirty."

"Well," I said, "I haven't seen you for a hell of a long time, and I'm in no damn mood to waste any time talking to Franzie Ketch or anyone else," and she said, "Push, push, *push!* My God, it won't take all *night* to talk with Franzie," and I said, "Any God-damn time is too much," and she said, "Damn it to hell, Junior, can't you get it through your head that Franzie can be important to you? Anyhow, he's damn sure as important to you as I am, because I told you before and I'll tell you again that I'm no lousy philanthropist to be trading time and talent for peanuts, and if you want to drop your shoes beside my couch any more you'd better believe me."

I said okay, okay, I'd see him, and she said, "Good for you, Junior," and hung up. I'd called her from Arnold Hamshank's

102

place, and I went in his office and said, "Who the hell's Francis Z. Ketch?" and he looked at me and said, "No one but the biggest gambler and crook in this town. Why?" and I said, "Oh, I just heard someone mention him like he was supposed to be pretty hot stuff and just wondered who he was, that's all," and as a matter of fact I'd been pretty sure he was something like that all along, and I was pretty sure how he'd want to put me in the way of making a potful, too, and I didn't know if we could work anything out about it, but it wasn't any skin off my tail just to go see, so I went.

It turned out he lived in a hell of a big apartment house over on one of the fancy boulevards, and Candy and I buzzed over there in the Crosley and went up about a God-damn mile in the elevator to the floor he lived on. Candy pushed a button beside the door and started a mess of chimes going off inside, and the last few seconds while we were waiting, she whispered, "Now act your damn age, Skimmer, for Christ's sake, because Franzie's no guy to stand for any cute stuff," and I said, "All right, God-damn it, I'll be a regular lousy angel," and just then the door was opened by no one but Francis Z. Ketch himself.

We went into a living room that was bigger than a barn and covered with a carpet up to your God-damn knees, and Candy said, "Skimmer this is Mr. Ketch. Skimmer's the one I told you about, Mr. Ketch," and this Ketch held out a hand and said, "How are you, Skimmer?" and I said I was fine, and as a matter of fact you could have slapped me ass over elbows with a feather, and this was because he didn't look any more like a big crook and gambler than old Bugs's grandmother, for instance. He was a little sawed-off bastard, to start with, not even as tall as Candy, and he was one of these plump guys with a round face that had rosy cheeks and a little red mouth like they paint on Kewpie dolls, and his hair was soft and pure white and combed back in little waves on both sides of a crummy center part, and his hands and feet were so God-damn little they looked like a woman's. He talked in this soft, prissy voice that made you think he might be a fairy, and he told us to come on in and sit down, which we did, and some spook wearing soup and fish came in then with some drinks on a tray and gave us each one.

"Well, Skimmer," Francis Z. Ketch said, "I understand from Candy that you're quite a persistent fellow," and I said if that meant trying to get what I wanted, I sure as hell was, and he smiled and said, "That's very commendable, and if Candy's one of the things you want, I also commend your good taste," and I said Candy was damn sure one of the things I wanted, all right, and I was in there trying all the time, but she'd been making it pretty tough for me for some damn reason or other, and he laughed and made a little tent with his fingers over his pot gut and said, "Well, Candy's quite a popular young lady, and I'm afraid she's been spoiled, and indeed I feel impelled to warn you that if you expect to remain in favor you must be prepared to stand considerable expense."

That sounded to me like an invitation to take the God-damn bull by the horns, so I did and said, "Well, that's why I'm here, because Candy said you might be able to put me in the way of making a potful," and he smiled with his stinking little rosebud of a mouth and said, "You're certainly a direct young man, I'll say that for you," and then he sat there looking at me with these round blue eyes that looked so damn innocent you wouldn't have believed it, and as a matter of fact they reminded me of old Mopsy Beacon when she was talking about saving it.

I didn't say anything because I couldn't think of a damn thing to say, and pretty soon he said, "As a matter of fact, there *are* definite prospects for a young man in your position, provided he's willing to cooperate in certain essential matters," and I said, "You mean about the basketball?" and he said to Candy, "How refreshingly *direct* this fellow is," and to me, "Yes, about the basketball," and I said, "You mean to throw some games so you can make a potful betting against us like Gravy Dummke wanted to?" and he made a little face like something was hurting him and closed his eyes and said, "Oh, no, no, *no!* I have no idea who this Dummke person is, but I have nothing so crude in mind. You see, it's merely the matter of the spread."

I said I didn't know exactly what the hell he meant, and he said, "What I mean is, betting is done on the spread of points between the scores of the two teams. To illustrate, if Pipskill was favored to win by, say, ten points, I could bet on a closer score—take the other team and nine, for example—and thereby stand to win a considerable sum," and I said, "You mean we wouldn't even have to lose the game?" and he said, "Oh, gracious, no," and that's no damn lie, he really said oh, gracious, and I thought about it and said, "Well, to tell the God-damn truth, I don't even see anything particularly wrong in just missing a few to keep the score a little closer," and he sighed and said, "Personally I share your practical view of the matter, but I must say that many people do not, the authorities among them, and if we were to come to some agreement and it became noised about, I would be in more trouble than I care about, and you would be in a great deal more than I."

Well, I wasn't so God-damn thick that I couldn't recognize a threat when I heard it, even if he said it in the same voice he'd have used to ask the time of day, and the funny thing was, you wouldn't have thought it would have scared a lousy Brownie, coming like it did from a guy who looked like a cross between Santa Claus and a pansy, but as a matter of fact I got a little cold spot inside me and knew what he meant what he said and a hell of a lot more than he said, as far as that goes, and maybe I got that feeling from him just because he *was* such a gentle looking little bastard and said these things so quietly with his little red mouth smiling all the God-damn time. Anyhow, I said I wasn't fool enough to go around beating my chops about something like that, and besides I didn't think it would work, because old Micky Spicer was a damn good sharpshooter himself and might run the score up in spite of everything I could do, and he rubbed his hands together and said, "That's a very astute observation and shows you have your wits about you. I'm familiar with Spicer's record, just as I'm familiar with yours, and you are undoubtedly correct. Tell me, do you know your teammate well?"

I said we were roommates and old buddies, and he said, "Do you suppose you could influence him to enter into a three-party agreement?" and I said I wouldn't put it past him, and he said, "Good. Suppose you negotiate it," and I said I wouldn't be seeing Micky until school started, and he said that would be time enough and I could inform him of results through Candy, and then he stood up to let us know it was time we were getting the hell out, and at the door he said, "You will not

105

use my name with Spicer until he's committed, of course," and I said I wouldn't, and Candy and I went on around to her apartment and had some drinks and some fun, and it was almost four o'clock when she threw me out.

Well, after I'd seen Francis Z. Ketch that first time, I didn't see him again all the rest of the summer, but I kept seeing Candy whenever she figured it was my time on the schedule, which wasn't often enough by a damn sight, the way I looked at it, and she kept telling me that Ketch was counting on me to set things up with Micky whenever school opened again, and I said he didn't have to worry about it any, and if I knew old Micky like I thought I did he'd be right in there with his shoes off when it came to earning another buck. I kept on working for Arnold Hamshank, too, but there wasn't really a hell of a lot of work to it, and about a week before time for school to start I quit the job and checked out at the hotel and went on back out to the frat house at Pipskill and got settled. When I left, Arnold Hamshank shook my hand and told me what a privilege it had been to do something for one of the boys on the team and to be sure to stop in and see him now and then, and I said I would, and the truth is, I couldn't understand why anyone would be so God-damn crazy over someone just because he happened to play basketball, but I just thought it and didn't say it, you can bet dollars on that.

I was all set in the room when Micky got back, and it was pretty good to see the goofy bastard again, as a matter of fact, and I wondered if I ought to come straight out with the Francis Z. Ketch deal or wait around for a time that seemed just right for it, and finally I decided to wait because you couldn't always figure just how old Micky would take one thing or another, and he was a crazy bastard, like I said, and that's the truth of it. Meanwhile, over a month went by, and I went into town three or four times and had some fun with Candy, and the last time I went she said, "How you coming with this Micky Spicer?" and I said, "What you mean, how am I coming?" and she said, "You know damn well what I mean. Is he going to play ball or not?"

"Well," I said, "the truth is, I've been sort of waiting for the right time to ask him and haven't got it done yet," and she said, "In case you're interested, you damn well better *get*

106

it done because basketball season's getting pretty close and Franzie Ketch wants to know what he's got to look forward to, and he told me to tell you," and I said, "Well, you can tell Franzie from me to keep his God-damn drawers on," and she said, "Oh, sure, I'll tell him, Junior, and while we're on the subject, it might interest you to know that I'll damn well be keeping *mine* on, too, as far as you're concerned, if you foul up and miss out on the heavy sugar."

If you think she didn't mean it, you're crazy, and I knew damn well she meant it, so I went back out to Pipskill with the idea of putting it right up to old Micky, and as it turned out, it happened to be the right time I'd been waiting for, anyhow, and this is the way it was. He was flopped on the bed in the room when I went in, and he was grumbling to himself about something, and I said, "What the hell's the matter with you?" and he said, "In case you want to know, I'm just God-damn sick of being stony at least half the time, that's all."

I could see right away that I'd never find a better time to come in with Francis Z. Ketch, and I said, "What the hell brought *this* on?" and he said, "Oh, nothing, nothing at all, except I've got a chance to make hay with a sweet doll, and damned if I'm not broke, and everyone else seems to be, too, and I can't borrow a damn dime," and I said, "Well, don't look at me, I don't have any God-damn money," which was a damn lie, because I had some, and he said, "I sure as hell wish I could find a way to turn a few extra bucks. That hundred a month was all right for a lousy freshman, but a junior's got more expenses," and I said, "That's the damn truth if it was ever spoken," and then I stopped and looked at him, and he could see I had something on my mind, and pretty soon I said, "How'd you like to make some *big* dough and cut out this crap of borrowing a few stinking nickels and dimes until payday?" and he said, "How?" and I said, "Well, I know how I can put you in the way of it, if you're really interested."

He lay there on the bed and looked at me, and after a minute or two he said, "Bull! If you know so damn much about how to earn big dough, how come you haven't even got a lousy fin to loan me?" and I said, "Well, I only said I knew *how* to do it, I didn't say I was *doing* it, and to tell the truth, I can't get in on it myself unless you're willing to get in, too, and that's the damn truth," and he said, "I don't get you," and I said, "It's not so damn hard to get if you'll just pay attention, and as a matter of fact it only amounts to missing a few buckets now and then."

He rolled over on the bed and sat up on the edge and began to scratch around in his crummy hair that went every which way, and pretty soon he said, "You mean throw some games?" and I said, "Hell, no. You think I'd let dear old Pipskill down that way? We just miss enough to keep the score closer than the wise guys figured it, that's all," and he said, "It sounds dishonest to me," and I said, "Well, isn't that a crying damn shame! You sound like we'd have to *lose* the damn game or something. I told you we just missed enough to keep the score tight," and he shook his head and scratched in his crummy hair some more and said, "Just the same, I'll bet it's considered crooked," and I said, "Well, it may be considered crooked by a lot of unreasonable bastards, but what the hell of it, and the way I look at it is, it's not crooked unless you really *lose* the damn game."

He kept on sitting and scratching and thinking about it, and after a long time he said, "Who the hell's putting out this dough?" and I said, "A guy who's got it to put out, and that's damn well all you'll ever know unless you decide to come in," and he said, "How much would we get?" and I said, "I don't know yet, but it'll be plenty to start with and even more later because this is big time stuff, and make up your God-damn mind one way or the other because I don't intend to fool around with it forever, if you want to know the truth," and he said, "Okay, Skimmer, count me in," and I said, "Now you're being smart, and what's more, I just happen to remember an extra fin you can have to make hay with this damn doll, whoever she is."

The next day I called Candy and told her I had to see her about the deal, and she asked why I couldn't just tell her over the phone, but I said I'd rather not talk about it over the phone and if she didn't want to see me about it she could damn well wait until my turn on the schedule came up, and she said, "Jesus Christ, you've got more tricks up your sleeve than a card sharp. Well, come on downtown tonight and get it over with," so I went, and she was right, of course, and I

108

didn't mind talking about the deal over the phone at all but just wanted to get in an extra turn, which I did.

I went to the Gay Gander and had some drinks and shot the bull a little with Hershell Goans, and at eleven Candy came on to sing in a dress that damn near wasn't there, and it's the truth that I was pretty crazy about her and never got tired of her or wanted anyone else all the time I knew her, no matter how many extra turns I managed to get in. After she was finished, she went back to her room to change clothes, and everyone kept clapping for a while to get her to come back and sing some more, though mostly the guys probably just wanted to look at her, but she was pretty snotty about things like that and wouldn't sing any longer than her half hour even if they beat their damn hands off. We had a drink together at the bar and went out to the Crosley and around to her apartment, and when we were up there she said, "Well, what's the big news?" and I said, "Nothing except old Micky's coming in," and she said, "Why in hell couldn't you have just said so over the phone?" and I said, "Well I *could* have said so, as a matter of fact, but there are other things you can't do over a telephone," and she threw her hands up in the air and said, "My God, Junior, you're so *insatiable*," which I found out later was just a way of saying I was hard as hell to satisfy.

She wasn't sore, though, and as a matter of fact she wasn't so damn easy to satisfy herself, and we wound up having some fun, and afterward she said, "Listen, Junior, you may not know it but Franzie Ketch owns the Gay Gander, and a lot of other people know it, even if you don't, so now that you've closed your deal with him you better not come there any more," and I said, "Why the hell not?" and she said, "If you're so damn dumb you can't see the reason, there's no use trying to explain it. Just don't come, that's all."

I could see the reason, all right, and said, "Well, where the hell shall I meet you when it's my turn on the schedule?" and she said, "What's the matter with this place?" and I said, "Not a damn thing as a matter of fact," and she said, "*All right*, then. Now get the hell out of here and let me get some sleep," and I did.

Out at Pipskill we started basketball practice, and you'd have thought after damn near seven months that old Umplett

109

would have forgotten how we'd got our butts tromped in the national finals the season before just because the other team happened to be better than pistols, but I can damn sure tell you he *hadn't* forgotten it, and he was sour and mean and had blood in his eye, and the truth is, he seemed to hate the guts of everyone on the team, especially mine, and I don't mind admitting that I began to get a hell of a bang out of thinking how I was fooling him by being set up with Francis Z. Ketch to make something on the side. He worked the hell out of us, and if you fumbled a pass or missed a shot or slowed down under ninety miles an hour in the God-damn firehorse game we played, he'd stop the action and chew you out in that quiet way of his that was somehow a hell of a lot worse than if he'd bellowed at you like old Mulloy or someone, and all the time he was chewing he'd be looking at you with his little eyes all sick and sour in their sockets and his lips working around like his words had a lousy taste in his mouth, and if you want to know what I think, I think the son of a bitch was crazy, and in fact I'd bet on it.

He was a good coach, though. Like I said before, he was a damn good coach, and I can't deny it. We got fast and slick and better than we'd been the year before, and even old Carboy smoothed out and got a little better with the hook, and when we had our first warmup game about a week after the football team wound up in the cellar as usual, there must have been fifteen thousand maniacs piled into the field house to see the team that everyone thought would be national champs sure this year, and certain people damn well knew we'd *better* be, including us and old Umplett, and after the game everyone thought so more than ever, especially the team we played, because we murdered them. After that we played another team that wasn't any match for us, and then an outfit from the East breezed in on tour, and they were experienced and supposed to be damn good, and it turned out that this was the first game that Francis Z. Ketch wanted me and Micky to fix the point spread in. It was Candy who called me to pass the word, and I'll tell you how it was.

I was at the frat house, and this guy called up from downstairs and said, "Telephone, Scaggs," and I went down and answered, and it was Candy, and she said, "Hello, Junior.

110

Well, it's your turn on the schedule," and I said, "I'm damn glad to hear it, but it's the first time you ever called me to tell me so, and I'd like to know why," and she laughed and said, "Not my schedule, Junior. Franzie Ketch's schedule. You better come on downtown tonight and get the details," and I said, "Well, since I've got to come downtown anyhow, you might as well work your schedule around to fit Franzie's," and she said, "Lord God, you can figure more angles than any engineer. Remember to come right to my place and not to the Gay Gander," and I said I would and did.

I got there before she did and had to wait in the hall, and I made up my mind right then if I was going to have to meet her that way, not knowing just when she'd get there, I'd have to have a key to the joint so I could go on in and make myself comfortable. She came along after a while and said, "Hi, Junior," and we went in and had a drink, and she said, "I guess I'll have to quit giving you drinks now that you're playing basketball again," and I said, "The hell you will! You just let me worry about the God-damn basketball," and she said, "Well, you can start worrying about the game Saturday night, because Franzie Ketch says the wise money is going for you to win by eight points on your home court, but he figures it will be closer," and I said, "How closer?" and she said, "The way he sees it, not over seven."

Well, that's how it was, the way we settled it, and I started to get down to other business, and she said, "How the hell do you expect to keep on being a star athlete with the kind of habits you've got?" and I said she could damn well quit bothering herself about it, and after a while she did, and when I was finally ready to get on back out to Pipskill, I remembered about having to wait in the hall and said, "By the way, you better get a key made for me," and she asked me what the hell I meant, a key, and I said, "A key to open the God-damn door with. You think I want to stand out in the lousy hall waiting every time you're late?" and she said, "Well, of all the lousy damn brass I ever heard of, this takes the prize. I'll just tell you, Junior, that you can wait in the hall or in hell or any place you damn well please, but if you think you're getting a key to my apartment you can put it out of your little mind right now," and I could see that she was really in an uproar about it for some

111

God-damn reason or other, so I let it drop for the time being, but I didn't put it out of my mind, like she said, but intended to come back to it later because I couldn't see any sense whatever in waiting around for her in the damn hall.

I went back to the frat house and told Micky how it had been set, and he said, "It oughtn't to be very hard to make it look good at seven points because this team's supposed to be pretty sharp," and I said, "Well, we damn well *better* make it look good because I've got a feeling old Umplett will smell something damn fast if we don't," and Micky said, "That's for sure, and I don't mind admitting that the son of a bitch gives me the creeps," and I said that went for me, too, doubled in spades.

The truth is, we damn near flubbed it. It was the other team's fault, really, the bastards, because they didn't come through the way they were supposed to, and the way it was, they played sharp and fast the first half and kept within four points all the way, which was the widest spread we built, but then, the second half, damned if they didn't grow all feet and thumbs and get as cold as a damn ice cube, and almost before we knew it we had a lead of twelve points. I got worried as hell, and that's the truth, and during a time out I whispered to Micky to start missing some, for God's sake, and he whispered back, "Well, damn it, it's not so much our *missing* some as figuring a way to get those spooks to start *hitting* some," and I had to admit to myself that he had a damn good point.

To make it worse, that God-damn Carboy had a good night and even hooked in a few, and Micky and I had to look so damn bad to make up for it that I got to worrying about old Umplett jerking us out of there, and then we wouldn't have had any chance at all to fix the spread. In the fourth quarter, though, the other team got its eye back and began to move the ball better, and with the help of Micky and me they got the spread narrowed to six points with less than a minute to play, and it looked like everything would come out all right after all, and it was right then that the thing happened that looked pretty God-damn phony, and I'll have to admit it.

The other team had the ball and took it downcourt and banged away at the basket and missed, and old Carboy went up and took it off the boards and passed it out, and we took it down in no hurry because we had the game on ice, and ordinarily we'd have just hung onto the ball until the gun. They were playing a man-for-man defense, though, and the guy on me got sloppy and dropped away, and old Carboy in the slot got the ball and popped it out to me, and there I was in the open with the God-damn ball and plenty of time to dribble in and lay one up that would have been as easy as hitting a bull with a spade. To tell the truth, I didn't know what the hell to do, and so I wound up not doing a damn thing, and the spook who was supposed to be guarding me woke up and got in between me and the basket, and it looked pretty phony, like I said, and as a matter of fact it stank.

The gun went off then, and we went in the locker room, and when I came out of the shower and started dressing, old Umplett came out of his office and looked at me with his sour, sick eyes and said, "Why the hell didn't you go in for that last shot?" and I'd been thinking he might ask me about it and had a reason ready for him, so I said, "Well, we were ahead and only had a few seconds to go, and I thought there wasn't any use in it."

He kept on looking at me, and his lips sort of curled back off his crummy teeth in a little smile that didn't have any God-damn humor in it at all, and pretty soon he said in this very soft voice, "Well, isn't that just too God-damn touching for words! If there's anything makes me want to break right out in tears, it's a guy like you who has such a tender heart that he just can't stand beating anyone any worse than's absolutely necessary. I've been at this business a long time, and sometimes I get to feeling pretty low and thinking maybe it's been a wasted life and I've never done anyone in the world any good to speak of, and then a fine, tender-hearted lad like you comes along and makes me feel ashamed of feeling and thinking that way. However, we got to remember to be realistic about things, and one of the things we got to remember is that there's a time to hold the ball and run out the clock, and there's a time when it's better to take a shot, especially when it's a dead cinch to make and not even enough time left for the other team to get the ball back downcourt. I don't have to tell you this, though, because you're a natural sharpie and know damn well when to shoot and when not to, and you

113

knew you should've taken that shot tonight. I don't know why you didn't, except for the natural tenderness of your heart, and I don't want to know, but I can God-damn well tell you that if you ever pull another phony trick like that while you're playing on this team I'll make you sorry you were ever born, and don't you forget it."

Well, I could see the son of a bitch didn't trust me and was going to be suspicious of every lousy little thing I did, and I knew damn well I'd have to smooth it up and do better if I ever intended to get away with it and had just about decided to tell Francis Z. Ketch to blow it when I got a call from Candy to come downtown to her apartment and pick up something she had for me. I went down there in the Crosley to pick it up, and it was the payoff for fixing the spread, and as a matter of fact it was five hundred for me and three for Micky, and I got the extra two for setting it up and being the contact man, which was just adding sauce to the gravy, the way I looked at it, since the one I had to contact was Candy and she usually had something extra for me herself.

She gave me the money and said, "Well, how does it feel to be in the chips?" and I thought I might as well push it a little while I was at it and said, "It feels pretty damn good, all right, but Francis Ketch doesn't need to think I'm going to keep on fixing points for any lousy five C's per, and you can tell him from me it'll have to go up a couple of C's each time," and she looked at me with her eyes wide for a few seconds and then said, "By God, you might be worth hanging onto, at that, if you can manage to keep living," and I said, "Don't worry about that, and while we're on the subject of living, how about living it up a little right now?" and she laughed and shook her head and said, "Probably someday I'll wonder why I was ever so damn crazy, but just the same I think you're pretty cute, Junior, and I'm tempted to cooperate." Which she did.

I went back out to Pipskill pretty late, and the next day I slipped Micky the three hundred, and it bucked him up some and made him feel like going on with the deal with Francis Z. Ketch, and the truth is, he'd been pretty shaky about it and inclined to give it up. The first part of December, about the tenth, we took off on a tour, and this time we swung west instead of east. There wasn't any worry about fixing the spreads, of course, because Francis Z. Ketch couldn't keep in contact, and we let ourselves go and won all five of the games we played by big scores, except one that was close in California, and by the time we got back, Pipskill was already being voted number one team in the country, and I was way out in front personally in individual scoring. I might as well tell you right off that the team and I both stayed right there all season, in spite of my having to miss a few on purpose in some games, and as a matter of fact I got a lot of attention in the sports pages and had my picture in about six national magazines, two times in color, and was called the Pipskill Flash and the Pipskill Ace and other things like that.

We got back to Pipskill and laid off until after Christmas, and then we won two home games with the spreads fixed, and they worked out a lot smoother than the first one, and I didn't get the two C's more each game, but I did get one C more, which was as much as I'd expected, anyhow. The only thing that bothered me was that God-damn Umplett, and I kept thinking he was looking at me and watching me and crap like that, but I decided it was just because I had him on my lousy mind all the time, and finally I put him out of it, and damned if I didn't feel better right away.

Right after that, just when I was feeling free and easy and loose as ashes about it all, the whole thing started going to hell and it seems like that's the way things go sometimes, just all to hell and nothing you can do about it, but anyhow, I guess I'd better get into it and tell how it happened. It was all that God-damn Micky's fault, and I don't mind saying he had me fooled all the way, and I never even suspected that he'd play me the dirty trick he did. We started conference play and won a couple of games away from home, and I noticed he didn't play up to par and made a hell of a lot of mistakes he didn't usually make, but I didn't think much about it because everyone gets off his game now and then, and the truth is, it was the way he started acting in the room at the frat house that finally made me wonder what the hell was itching him. He acted like a spook, I mean, like he had a God-damn belly-ache or something, and finally one night I tried to get a little chatter going with him about this and that, and he

115

wouldn't say much but acted like he wished to hell I'd get away and leave him alone, so I said right out, "What the hell's the matter with you, anyhow? As far as I can see, you're about as gay as a pregnant spinster."

He said, "I been meaning to talk with you about it, Skimmer, and the truth is, I'm pretty damn miserable," and I said, "What the hell you got to be miserable about?" and he sighed like he had a God-damn pain and said, "You remember the girl I told you about? The one I borrowed the fin to make hay with?"

I said I did, and he said, "Well, I didn't make any hay, and as a matter of fact I ought to have my tail kicked for even thinking about it because this girl doesn't go for stuff like that and has extremely high standards," and I hooted and said, "Well, pass the God-damn collection plate!" and he got red in the face and a stubborn look in his eyes and said, "No bull, Skimmer, I've really got it bad over this girl, and she's got it bad over me, and the truth is, we've been talking about getting married and everything," and I said, "Well, if you've got to get married to get it, you better go ahead and get married, but I don't see why the hell it should give you gas on the stomach just to think about it," and he said, "It's not that, Skimmer. The thing that's wrong, it's this deal we got to fix the spreads in the basketball games. If Helen ever found out about it, she wouldn't have a damn thing more to do with me because she's got these God-damn high standards, and besides, if you want to know it, I'm beginning to feel kind of dirty about it myself, and I wish I'd never got started at it as a matter of fact."

I could see right away that it was pretty damn serious, and I don't mind admitting that it scared the hell out of me, and I said, "I don't know anything about how damn dirty you're feeling, but I can tell you one thing, and that is that this Helen, whoever she is, damn well better *not* find out anything about it," and he said, "Oh, I wouldn't tell her, of course," and I said, "Besides, you been getting paid pretty good for helping fix the spread, and I'll bet Helen's been getting her share of it one way or another, and what's more, I'll bet she didn't bother to ask whether it was dirty or not," and this made him sore, and he stood up and stuck out his stinking chin and said, "You lay off Helen or I'll knock your God-damn teeth out," and I

116

laughed and said, "Lay off, hell! It looks to me like a guy can't even lay *on!*"

When I said that, he flipped his lousy lid and swung at me and missed and I swung at him and hit and knocked him back across the God-damn bed, and he bounced up and came back at me, and altogether we made so damn much noise that a couple of guys from the next room ran in and pulled us apart, and one of them said, "What the hell's going on? What the hell's the matter with you guys?" We couldn't tell the truth, as you can see, so I lied and said it was nothing much, just a little disagreement, but now we had it out of our God-damn systems and everything would be all right. They patted us on the backs and said sure, they knew how it was and everything, and pretty soon they got out and went back to their own crummy room, but it wasn't all right, not by a damn sight, and I knew right then he was going to play me a dirty trick, and I should've had my head examined for trusting him another God-damn minute.

I thought about it and wondered how to get him back to being the same old Micky, and one of the things I thought of was to go and find this Helen and make her or something and break it up between them, but I wasn't sure it would work out just right, because you never can tell exactly how a guy will react to having his girl made by a friend, and besides, to tell the truth, I had Candy on my mind and couldn't put my heart in it. Anyhow, as it turned out, I wouldn't have had time, because there was a heavy non-conference game coming up, and the night before the game Candy called me and told me to come downtown, and I went, and she said, "Franzie can take this team and seven and get plenty of takers, so he says for you to keep it under that," and I said I'd try.

She said, "What the hell you mean, try?" and I said, "I mean there may be complications in it," and she said, "Junior, you don't know anything about complications until you foul up on one of these deals. Explain yourself. What the hell you mean, complications?" and I told her about how old Micky had been set on his tail by this Helen doll, and how he was thinking about backing out on his agreement with Francis Z. Ketch because of it, and Candy said, "Believe it or not, Junior, I wouldn't want you to get hurt in this thing, in spite of feeling personally that it would do you good to get slapped around a little, and so maybe we'd better get in touch with Franzie and get you off the hook ahead of time just in case something goes wrong."

"Well," I said, "I sort of hate to put the finger on old Micky right now because I've got an idea he may come out of it, and anyhow, I'm pretty damn sure I can talk him into sticking one more game at least," and she said, "It's your funeral, Junior, and don't expect me to send flowers," and I said, "You talk like I'm practically in the God-damn morgue or something."

She said, "Famous last words, Junior," and I said, "Well, in that case, I'd better start living up what's left to live in a hurry," and she said, "My God, we went through *that* routine the last time you were here. I'd think you'd be absolutely *limp!*" but the truth is, she didn't think any such damn thing and was pretty good at living it up herself, and that's the big reason we hit it off so damn good, and in my opinion it's a crying shame it had to end up the way it did, which I'll tell about, and all because that damn Micky had to go off the deep end over a doll who was all cluttered up with high standards and stuff like that.

I didn't have a chance to talk to Micky the next day, and as a matter of fact I didn't have a chance to talk to him until we were in the locker room in the field house just before the game. I got him in a corner and told him how the spread was fixed and what it was supposed to be, and the son of a bitch just looked at me with his eyes all snotty and didn't say a damn word, and I had a feeling right then that he was going to do me the dirty, and damned if he didn't. I don't intend to go into it much because, to tell the truth, it's sort of painful to remember, and I don't like to think about it, but I could tell from the beginning that the bastard was out to make it a big night, and the worst of it was, he happened to be hot and couldn't miss and was popping the damn ball through the bucket from all angles. The other team called a time out after a while, and I whispered to Micky, "What the hell you trying to do, you crazy bastard?" and he looked at me with these snotty eyes and said, "Go to hell," and I said, "You'll think go to hell if you get fouled up with Francis Z. Ketch," and he said, "Francis Z.

Ketch can go to hell, too, as far as I'm concerned," and I knew I'd had it, and there was nothing I could do about it.

I kept on trying, though, and wouldn't pass to the bastard even when I saw him open for a shot, but old spooky Carboy kept feeding them to him from the slot, and as a matter of fact I had to look so damn bad trying to keep the score down that old Umplett finally jerked me, the son of a bitch, and it was the first time I'd ever been jerked except once in a while for a short rest. He wouldn't even look at me when I went over and sat down on the bench, but I could tell he was smelling something and hating my guts, and I rode the God-damn bench the rest of the game, and I won't tell you the final score but will just say that the spread was a hell of a lot too wide to win any money for Francis Z. Ketch, and as a matter of fact lost him a hell of a potful. The God-damn maniac spectators were going crazy and raising hell, and the lousy band started playing what they called the victory march, but from my point of view there was damn little to celebrate, and I went in the dressing room feeling lower than a snake's belly and wondering if Francis Z. Ketch could blame me for what had happened, even if it wasn't my God-damn fault whatever.

I showered and got dressed in a hurry, and I was sitting on the bench by my locker putting on my lousy shoes when Micky came up and looked down at me and said, "Now what do you think?" and I looked up at him and said, "I'll tell you what I think. I think you're a dirty, double-crossing son of a bitch, but you better quit worrying about what I think and start worrying about what Francis Z. Ketch thinks, and I wouldn't be in your shoes for all the God-damn dolls with high standards between here and Texas," and as a matter of fact I didn't even particularly like the idea of being in my own shoes, but I didn't say so.

He turned and walked away without saying anything more, and the next morning he moved all his crummy stuff to another room in the frat house, and as far as I was concerned it was good riddance of bad rubbish, as the saying goes. I kept thinking all day I'd get some kind of word from Candy about how Francis Z. Ketch was feeling about the way the game came out, and I cut all my stinking classes just to hang around

119

the phone, but I didn't hear a damn word. I went to basketball practice when the time came, and old Umplett didn't have a damn word to say, either, which was a relief, and when I got back, the guys at the house said there still hadn't been any call for me, and I was just about to decide that Francis Z. Ketch was going to be reasonable about it when the phone rang, and it was Candy, and she said, "You better get down to my apartment in a hurry, Junior," and I got in the Crosley and went.

When I got there, she opened the door and let me in, and I said, "Hi, doll," and she said, "You forget the schedule, Junior. This is strictly business," and I looked past her and saw no one but Francis Z. Ketch himself in a chair and knew that it damn well was. He had his little hands folded across his pot and this little smile on his stinking little mouth, and he said, "Well, Skimmer, it seems there's been a misunderstanding," and I said, "Well, it wasn't exactly a God-damn misunderstanding," and he said, "You can call it what you like, but I lost a great sum of money, which disturbs me greatly, and I'll confess that there's nothing in the world disturbs me quite so much as losing a great sum of money, especially when it's due to the defection of a trusted associate."

I didn't quite get the meaning of all the words, but I damn well got the *general* meaning, you can bet your butt on that, and I got this God-damn cold feeling that he gave you with his soft voice and his stinking little red smiling mouth, and I said, "Well, I did my damnedest to keep the spread down, and even got jerked out of the game for looking so lousy doing it, and the truth is, that damn Micky Spicer met a girl with high standards and wouldn't have any part of it," and he said, "Are you suggesting that Spicer refused to cooperate?" and I said, "Well, if you've got any doubts, you can look at the God-damn box scores in the paper, and I'm not suggesting a damn thing but saying it right out."

He sat there looking at me and started flipping his crummy underlip with one finger like he was thinking about it, and after a while he said, "Why wasn't I informed in time to avoid this fiasco?" and I said, "To tell the truth, I didn't think he'd do me the dirty when it came right down to it, and I didn't find out for sure he was going to do it until the game started," and

120

he nodded and said, "I'm inclined to believe that you personally have been guilty of nothing more than stupidity, which was a calculated risk I accepted in the beginning. This Spicer fellow, however, seems to have pulled a deliberate double-cross. I haven't had the pleasure of meeting him yet, and I think it's time I had it. You can be of some assistance in the matter."

I said, "How's that?" and he said, "Why, you can simply persuade him to come downtown for the purpose," and I said, "The hell I can. He's got his nose hard and moved out of our room and won't have a damn thing to do with me, and I couldn't persuade him to take a new automobile as a gift," and he said, "Well, I can see how that might be true, under the circumstances. Perhaps, to avoid any further bungling, I'd better send Conky to get him. Conky is the most persuasive fellow at my command, and I'm sure he can convince Spicer that he shouldn't deny me the pleasure of meeting him."

He got up then and got his hat and said good-by and left, and he wasn't fooling me any with his polite talk and stinking little smile, not a damn bit, and I knew that whatever he had in mind for Micky might be a pleasure to him but none at all to Micky, and I felt a little bad about it and wished it didn't have to happen, but I didn't really figure it was any skin off my butt, after all, because the simple truth is, the son of a bitch brought it on himself and deserved it.

After Francis Z. Ketch was gone, Candy said, "Well, that was a close shave, Junior, and it's damn lucky you had a sucker," and I said, "It seems to me that I was the sucker, not getting a damn cent for this game in spite of trying my best, and it seems like the least you could do to make up for it would be to put me on the schedule for tonight," and she said, "Well, you may get slapped down now and then, but you sure bounce up in a hurry, I'll have to admit, and it might be a good idea to put you on the schedule, at that, because the way things are looking at the moment, it could damn well be your last turn," and as it happened, that's the way it turned out, and I wish it hadn't.

The next afternoon, Micky wasn't at practice, and I wondered about it but didn't say anything. I was feeling nervous as a whore in church, to tell the truth, and after practice was over I went and got something to eat in a joint and walked

121

around some and wound up in a stinking movie, and when I finally got back to the frat house it was pretty late, and no one but old Umplett himself was sitting in my room waiting for me. It scared the hell out of me to come onto him like that all of a sudden without any warning, him just sitting and looking at me with his God-damn sick eyes full of that damn unreasonable hate of his, and I said, "Well, hello, Coach," and he said, "Don't bother pretending to be glad to see me, and in fact don't even talk to me any more than's absolutely necessary," and I said, "What the hell's the matter?" and he said, "You know damn well what's the matter," and I said, "Like hell I do," and he said, "Well, in that case, just come along with me and I'll damn well show you."

I followed the sour son of a bitch downstairs and out to his car, and I didn't like it, and as a matter of fact I was a hell of a lot more worried than I'd ever been or intend to be again. He didn't say another damn word, and I didn't, either, and we rode downtown to a hell of a big building with a drive going up in front of it to a parking area, and we went up the drive and parked and got out, and I could see the building was a hospital. Well, I knew damn well what had happened then, that Francis Z. Ketch had had the pleasure of meeting Micky Spicer, though maybe it was more or less by proxy, as they put it, and whatever way they put it, it sure hadn't been any God-damn pleasure for Micky.

Old Umplett and I went inside and up in the elevator and down a hall to the room where they'd put old Micky, and I wouldn't even have recognized him if I hadn't known damn well who it was, and he was in bed with his head all in bandages like one of these God-damn sultans or something, and one arm in a cast and lying on top of the sheet that covered him, and I could see that he was in a hell of a bad way and wasn't even conscious, in fact. We stopped just inside the door and looked at him, and a nurse was beside the bed and came over and said, "No one is allowed in here for the present. I'm sorry but you'll have to leave," so we backed out in the hall, and I said, "What the hell happened to him?" and he looked at me with these damn eyes of his and said in this soft, sarcastic voice, "Oh, that's right. You don't know anyhing about it yet, do you? Well, I know Spicer was a buddy of yours and

122

that you're naturally worried all to hell about him, so I'll explain it to you. He was in an accident. He was wandering around down in one of those narrow streets near the river for some crazy reason or other, and he got smeared by a hit and run driver. The cops had a wild idea he'd been beaten up and thrown out of a car, but I managed to convince them it couldn't have been anything like that."

He stopped and stood looking down at the floor, and for a minute I had an idea he was going to spit, which would have been a hell of a thing to do in a hospital, but he didn't and then he looked up at me again and said very softly, "You see, it's like this. This year I got the national champs. This year I got the champs as sure as hell, and nothing, nothing in the God-damn world, is going to get in the way or stop us or keep us from *being* champs. It'll be tougher now than it might have been otherwise, because Spicer's got a busted arm and a fractured skull and won't play another game this season, but we'll be national champs just the same, and I'll tell you why. We'll be champs because of you, Scaggs. We'll be champs because you're a sharpshooting, ball-hawking natural, whatever else you are or aren't, and from now on you'll play basketball each game and every game like you never played it before, and if I get the idea you're letting me down one little bit, God save your soul!"

After he'd said that, he turned around and walked off down the hall, and damned if he didn't get in his lousy car and drive back to Pipskill and leave me to get back by myself the best way I could, and a taxi was the best way and cost me over two bucks. I'll have to admit I was in a damn sweat, and the truth is, I never met a guy who got under my skin any more than he did, not even Francis Z. Ketch. I was pretty sure he didn't know *exactly* what had happened, and didn't even *want* to know, but he damn well knew what had happened in a general kind of way, I wasn't kidding myself about that, and mostly what put me in a sweat was, it looked to me like I was in a crack between him and Ketch. I worried about it for three damn days, and finally I decided I'd talk to Candy about it, so I called her and said, "Hello, Candy, this is Skimmer," and she said, "Who?" and I said, "Skimmer, God-damn it. Skimmer Scaggs," and she said, "Look, Buster, you better

123

get a new routine. I don't know anyone named Skimmer Scaggs and never have."

Well, I was so God-damn surprised I couldn't find my damn tongue for a minute, and by the time I'd found it she'd hung up. I thought about it quite a while, until after basketball practice that afternoon, as a matter of fact, and the more I thought about it, her trying to kick me out of bed that way, the madder I got, and that evening I got in the Crosley and went downtown to the Gay Gander. It was still about twenty minutes before time for Candy's spot, so I climbed on a stool at the bar and ordered a highball and was just about to take a swallow when someone said, "Sorry, sonny, we don't serve minors in this bar," and I set the highball down on the bar and turned around on the stool, and it was Hershell Goans who had said it.

"What the hell you mean, minor?" I said, and he said, "A minor is a kid under twenty-one, sonny," and I said, "Well I've drunk about fifty gallons of your God-damn slop in here, and you never worried about how old I was before, and besides, I'm over twenty-one, and you know it damn well, and to be exact I'm twenty-three," and he said, "How the hell would I know how old you are? I don't know you from Adam's off ox. You got a birth certificate on you?" and I said, "Oh, sure, I carry a God-damn birth certificate around with me all the time, and don't give me any crap about not knowing me, either, because that's the same runaround Candy's trying to give me, and I'm here to find out why."

He showed his stinking teeth to me and said, "Look, sonny, don't try to tell me you're a personal friend of Candy Caldwell's," and I said, "Well, if I'm not, she's sure been giving a lot of good stuff to a stranger," and he clucked his crummy tongue against his teeth and said, "Shame on you, sonny, saying things like that about a nice girl like Candy Caldwell. Don't you know you could be sued for slander for saying things like that?" and I was getting pretty sick of his snotty attitude and said, "Well, I don't know a God-damn thing about being sued for slander, but I'll tell you what I do know. I know you're going to lose a handful of your God-damn teeth if you don't get off my back."

I could see that he was beginning to get riled up himself,

124

and he pulled in his teeth and smoothed out his face and said, "Look, sonny, I don't like nasty kids who come in here making threats and trying to make the entertainers. I ought to have you thrown right out on your tail, but I'm a kindly guy by nature and inclined to give you a break. Suppose you just step back to Miss Caldwell's dressing room with me, and we'll get this all straightened out," and I said I sure as hell would, and we went through a door into a hall and down the hall to another door, and he knocked and said, "It's Hershell, Candy," and she said on the inside, "Come on in, Hersh."

He opened the door, and I went in ahead of him, and Candy was sitting at a dressing table fixing her face. She was wearing a white satin dress that wasn't a hell of a lot more than she'd worn on schedule, which wasn't a damn thing, and she looked up and saw me in the mirror, and it's a fact that you couldn't tell from her face that she'd ever seen me before. Hershell Goans said, "Here's a guy says he knows you, Candy," and she said to the mirror, "Lots of guys say they know me," and he said, "You ever seen him before?" and she said, "Never," I'm damned if she didn't, and he turned to me with his teeth out again and said, "There you are, Sonny. Satisfied?"

Well, I wasn't so damn dumb I didn't know what was coming off, and I'd known it the minute Candy gave me the works on the telephone, which was that Francis Z. Ketch had put out the word to cut me loose, and I said to Candy, "Well, I'm satisfied if you are, because you're nothing but a round-heeled bitch, and the truth is, I was beginning to get tired of it, anyhow," and that got under her skin and she jumped up and said, "Tired of it, hell! You couldn't get enough of it!" and I laughed and said, "I thought you'd never seen me before," and she said, "What a smart little bastard you are!" and Hershell Goans said, "Yeah. Too damn smart," and he'd slipped in behind me and grabbed my arm and bent it up behind my back, and it hurt like hell.

I tried to get loose, but every damn time I moved he'd shove up on my arm, and it felt like it was damn well coming out of the socket at the shoulder, and finally I got quiet and looked at Candy, and she said, "Look, Junior, as a Goddamn athlete you ought to know that all schedules end when the season's over, and the simple truth is, the season's over for you and me. I won't say it wasn't fun, and as a matter of fact I'll admit it was, but it wasn't enough fun to justify keeping it up when the percentage is out of it, and now that Franzie's goons have got too God-damn ambitious and brought the heat on, the percentage is damn well out of it. Right now the risk would be too big for the cut, and that means that you were useful once but aren't useful any more, and it's tough as hell and all that, but that's the way it is. In brief, Junior, it's just like I said to Hershell. I don't know you. I never saw you. Who the hell's Skimmer Scaggs?"

I could see that she was laying it on the line, all right, and that there wasn't a damn bit of use fighting it, but the truth is, she looked pretty slick in that white satin dress, and I didn't want to give up my turn on the schedule in spite of what I'd said to the contrary, but I sure as hell wasn't going to give her the satisfaction of knowing it, so I said, "Well, you may not know who Skimmer Scaggs is now, but you'll damn well know who he is before he's through, and everyone else in the damn country will know who he is, and that's a hell of a lot more than they'll ever know about a doll who doesn't do anything but diddle on a schedule and sing dirty songs in a joint," and then before Hershell Goans could push up on my arm again, I jerked away and turned and kicked him right where it did the most good and scooted out into the hall and down the alley, and from the God-damn noise in the room behind me, it sounded like the bastard's name should have been Hershell Groans instead of Hershell Goans. I went down the alley and around to the street where I'd left the Crosley, and all the way back to Pipskill I kept thinking about Candy and wishing the schedule hadn't ended, and as a matter of fact I still wish it, and it seems like I remember her more than any other doll I ever knew, unless possibly Marsha Davis.

Well, as I see it, there's not a hell of a lot of use going on with it much longer, except to say that Pipskill went all the way and got to be national champs, even without Micky Spicer, and afterward I was pretty tired of it, especially at nothing but a hundred a month, and decided to quit. I went ahead on the quiet and got lined up to play with a pro team, the team I'm still playing with, and then I went around to old Umplett's office in the field house and walked in and said, "Well, Coach, I've decided to quit old Pipskill, and I've just come around to tell you to blow it."

He was sitting at his desk in a swivel chair, and he swung around in it very slowly and looked at me a long time with those God-damn sour, sick eyes of his, and then he said very softly, "So you're running out. Well, I've been expecting it, and I'm not surprised, and it's God's own wonder that you stuck around as long as you did. But you made us national champs. It was mainly you, and I'll hand it to you, and you're welcome. I made *you*, and you made *us*, and we're even and quits and to hell with it. Go, and God go with you, Mr. Scaggs. I'll follow your career with interest, and I have no doubt at all that you'll be a shining star in the professional world, and God himself knows the satisfaction it will be to my soul to remember the part I had in the making of you."

Then he started to laugh, not out loud like a reasonable person, but so softly you could hardly hear it, like he was laughing at something in his own mind that he didn't even think was very funny, and I think the son of a bitch was crazy, if you want to know the truth of it, and I turned around and got the hell out of there.

And that's all I'm going to tell about. The last damn word. All I wanted in the first place was to tell how I got started and made something of myself, and now I've told it, and you can see for yourself that it was all because of this God-damn crazy game and nothing else.